"I know what I heard! A dog howled all night long. We both know what that means." The woman stamped her high heeled, fringed leather boot causing her dyed black pageboy to swing over her shoulders. Sawdust flurried around her and her companion. "Someone's going to die!"

Deputy Tempe Crabtree stared curiously at the two women. Despite the fact the last statement had been shouted, she was surprised none of the many people milling around the crowded fairgrounds took any notice. The Indians, the majority dressed in Native American clothing, were busy preparing for the opening ceremonies of the Pow Wow. Those who had come to observe the gala event were too entranced by the huge colorful gathering to pay attention to two women arguing.

Sergeant Guthrie had given Tempe the special assignment of keeping the peace at the Pow Wow. He hadn't put it into words, but she knew it was because of her own Yanduchi heritage. The Pow Wow was the first to be held in Dennison, the nearest city to her own small community of Bear Creek. The event had attracted not only the Indian population from Dennison and the nearby reservation, but from far away as well. The parking lot was filled with vehicles with license plates from many other states.

Tempe re-tucked the back of her sharply creased tan uniform shirt into her trousers and stepped closer to the arguing women. The older of the two shook a plump finger near the nose of the other.

"Katherine Davelos, you have no idea what you're talking about! What you heard was probably just a bunch of coyotes. Only an Indian can recognize such a sign...and may I remind you that you are only married to an Indian. You are not one yourself!" The woman spoke sternly but didn't raise her voice. Though acquainted with the speaker, Tempe only knew her name was Violet Celso and that she was revered as a leader by the local Indians. Full blooded Yanduchi, with her round, weathered face and short, plump body, Violet reminded Tempe of pictures she had of her grandmother.

Tempe guessed Violet was in her late thirties. Her dark brown hair had been lightly permed, and she wore it in a simple style brushed back from her broad forehead. She wore a traditional buckskin dress, decorated with leather fringe on the bodice, sleeves and hem.

"You're just afraid my Linda is going to win the Princess contest!" The angry Katherine puckered her deeply tanned and overly made-up face into an ugly sneer before spinning on her heels and marching away, kicking up another cloud of sawdust.

Tempe stepped nearer to Violet. "What was that all about?"

Violet smiled. "Hi, Deputy Crabtree, heard you were going to be here. What do you think about all this?" She gestured at the milling crowd. People were beginning to fill the bleachers surrounding the arena, while those in Indian garb seemed to be gathering together near tables that had been set up at the entrance.

"Quite impressive. Had no idea the Pow Wow would attract so many people. Who is that gal?" Tempe nodded toward the woman moving away from them, her tight-jean-encased hips swinging provocatively.

"Katherine Davelos is a wannabe in the worst sense of the word. She lives on the reservation with her husband and daughter. We've never gotten along too well, but ever since her daughter entered the Princess contest Katherine has been impossible. You'd think she and I were competing against each other instead of my Marella and her Linda."

"What was that about someone dying?" Tempe automatically touched the silver barrette securing her long braid to the back of her head to make sure it was still in place.

"She probably meant that as a threat. When a dog howls all night for no reason, it may mean a death is imminent. She probably read that in a book. Pay no attention to Katherine. She's certainly irritating the way she prances around, pretending to be Indian. But she's harmless...harmless to everyone but that poor girl of hers."

Tempe raised a black eyebrow. "How do you mean?"

"She pushes Linda constantly. I doubt if the child even wanted to be in the contest."

"I'm afraid I don't know anything about this Princess business. Is it a beauty pageant?"

Violet chuckled. "Goodness no. If it were, my Marella would win easily, even if I do say so myself. The winner is the one who sells the most tickets for the drawing, so it's whoever works the hardest."

"Is there any reward besides the recognition?" Tempe asked.

"The recognition is the most important because the Princess becomes a role model for other young Indian women. She'll represent Dennison at a variety of events and speaking engagements all over California, including other Pow Wows. At the ceremony to present the new Princess, she'll receive a shawl, a jacket and a sash, and a beautiful beaded crown, along with a percentage of the ticket sales."

Tempe shook her head. "I had no idea there was so much involved with the Pow Wow."

"Yes, I've heard you don't know much about your heritage," Violet said.

"Who told you that?"

"Nick Two John."

Two John lived in Bear Creek. He'd been charged with murder earlier in the year, and Tempe had proven his innocence. Throughout her investigation, Two John had berated her for her lack of knowledge about the Yanduchi.

"I should have guessed," Tempe said.

"He organized this whole Pow Wow, you know."

"No, I didn't know. It looks like a lot of work."

"Most certainly. But a Pow Wow does a lot for our people. It's a way to teach our young folks about their culture and to portray a positive image to outsiders." Violet touched Tempe's arm. "I'd like to explain what's going to happen, but I don't have time. I've got to give the blessing to the dancers now."

While they'd been speaking, the crowd around the tables near the entrance to the arena had grown larger. Tempe watched as Violet moved among the costumed figures. She seemed to be waving smoke toward each individual. Tempe marveled at the diversity of the raiment. Though many were dressed in various versions of the traditional fringed buckskin dress and leggings, every kind of material imaginable from cotton, satin, and velvet had been fashioned into Indian garb and decorated with ribbons, beading, and feathers.

Because he was taller than most, Tempe noticed

Nick Two John above the crowd. The handsome Indian busily answered questions, waving his muscular arms; obviously in charge. As usual, he wore his long ebony hair parted in the middle and combed into two braids. Though she couldn't see much more than his shoulders, he seemed to be wearing a vest of some sort over his naked, broad chest.

The sound of a familiar female voice raised in anger caused Tempe to whirl around. Near the many booths where Indian crafts, memorabilia, and souvenirs were being sold, four young women stood. Katherine Davelos vehemently scolded one of them.

Straight brown hair falling from turquoise and coral studded barrettes hid the face of the object of the harangue, as the plump girl kept her head lowered. She wore a green satin dress with white fringe and white knee high leather moccasins.

The most beautiful of the group put her arm around the one Tempe knew must belong to Katherine, and said soothingly, "But it's time for all of us to line up for the processional, Mrs. Davelos."

"Of course you'd say that, Marella. You just want more time to sell your tickets without any competition from Linda." Katherine's blue eyes flashed hatred directed at Marella Celso.

"Mother, please." Linda protested weakly without lifting her head.

Violet was right, if the contest had been judged on beauty alone her daughter most certainly would have won. Marella's mahogany, hip-length hair had a freshly brushed sheen. Her large, nearly black eyes were filled with sympathy for Linda. The white gown with a colorfully beaded top, emphasized her slim figure.

The other two Princess contestants uncomfortably shifted their moccasined feet in the sawdust.

Retaining her composure and keeping her arm around Linda, Marella said, "That's not so, Mrs. Davelos. My mother is already doing the smoke blessing. It's time for us to get in line. You don't want Linda to miss being in the processional and not be seen by everyone in the grandstand, do you?"

Marella had obviously said the right thing. Katherine yanked her daughter from Marella's embrace and rubbed at an invisible smudge on her daughter's flat cheek. "The minute you're done with that folderol, you get yourself into circulation. Go back through the grandstands to sell your tickets."

"Come on, let's hurry," one of the other girls said, her braids thickened by ribbons, their bright ends trailing against the back of her midnight blue velvet gown. She started to run. The others followed quickly with Marella looking back and holding out a hand to encourage Linda to follow.

Katherine made shooing motions to hurry her daughter along.

Deciding to get closer in order to see what was going to happen in the arena, Tempe began edging her way around the assembled dancers and behind the tables. She wished she'd encouraged her son to come, but Blair hadn't shown much interest when she'd mentioned where she'd be spending her entire Saturday.

Tempe had raised her son alone after her highway patrolman husband was killed while chasing a suspect. Bringing her then two-year-old son with her, she'd returned to the tiny mountain community where she'd been raised. She and Blair made their home in a small cottage beside Bear Creek. In June, they'd been joined by Tempe's new husband, Hutch Hutchinson, the pastor of Bear Creek Community Church.

A senior in high school, Blair, had welcomed having another male in the family. Because Tempe usually worked evenings, Hutch and Blair saw more of each other than she did either of them.

As she made her way near the arena she could see that groups of men, young and old, were gathered around large drums situated at intervals around the inside perimeter with one drum in the center. Some of the men were dressed in regalia, others were more plainly attired in every-day clothing.

"Deputy Crabtree. Saw you mixing with the crowd a bit ago." Nick Two John stuck out his hand and grasped hers tightly. "How's the new marriage working out?"

"Wonderfully. Thought you and Claudia might be joining our ranks soon." Nick lived with his employer, Claudia Donato, who owned the Bear Creek Inn.

Nick shook his head, his dark eyes twinkling. "Why

mess up something that's working great just the way it is. What do you think of the Pow Wow so far?"

"I've never seen so many Native Americans gathered in one place. This must have been quite an undertaking."

"A lot of work," Nick said. "When I was getting all the permits your Sergeant Guthrie told me that even though we have our own security I had to have a deputy on the grounds. I asked that you be given the job. Thought it might do you some good." He almost smiled.

"H'mmm, I owe the Sergeant an apology. I figured he gave me the assignment just because I'm part Yanduchi."

"Frankly, Tempe, we don't need a deputy. We have two men specially chosen to control and maintain order." He pointed out the stern faced men and identified them. One was small and wiry Jake Celso, Violet's husband and Marella's father; the other, barrel-chested Abel Contreras.

"Any time you have thousands of people gathered in one place like this, there's potential for trouble," Tempe said, glancing around.

"There won't be any trouble, Deputy. We don't allow any drinking or drugs. And we don't tolerate profanity or rude behavior." Nick crossed his muscular arms over his chest. "A pow wow is a spiritual time. It's a celebration to give thanks, to honor our friends and elders, a time of music and dance."

The drums began to beat. Expectancy and eagerness crackled through the crowd as it slowly quieted. On the small grandstand, the master-of-ceremonies, an older Indian, wearing well-worn jeans, scuffed cowboy boots, a denim shirt and leather vest stepped up to the microphone.

After a short welcome, he went over the etiquette of the Pow Wow in a solemn manner. To those who came just to observe, he said, "The chairs in the arena are reserved for the judges. Before taking a picture of someone, permission must be granted. Do not enter the arena to take pictures. Do not touch anyone's dance regalia without asking first."

He then addressed the Indians participating in the ceremony. "Only those with permission from the Lead Singer may sit at the Drum. If you aren't wearing traditional regalia, you may only dance during the social songs.

"Singers, report to your drums. We will begin with the Gourd Dance."

The drum beat became steady and louder. Though Tempe hadn't noticed them enter, a large group of men now sat in a big circle inside the arena. They were dressed similarly, with red and blue cloth around their necks or draped over the right shoulders, with bandoleers of mescal beans worn over the left shoulder. Unable to see exactly what they were, she noticed decorations fastened to the middle of the red and blue blankets centered in the back. Some looked like military medals and ribbons.

Velvet sashes of either red or blue with fringe and beadwork on the ends encircled their waists. Each dancer held a gourd rattle in one hand and a feather fan in the other.

The drum beat continued, and a singer began. The men remained seated, shaking their rattles and feathers in time to the song. The dancers rose in unison and began moving in place, shaking the rattles and flexing their knees in time with the drum.

Jake Celso shoved his way through those waiting in the front of the line. A murmur of protest rose. Violet reached out toward her husband. "For goodness sake, Jake, what are you...."

Ignoring her, he darted around the end of the bleachers. Fearing trouble, Tempe quickly excused her way through the crowd. When she was free, she broke into a run in an attempt to catch up with Jake.

She found him standing at the other end of the bleachers, scratching his head. "What's going on?" she asked.

"I thought I saw someone who's got no business being here," Jake said, a frown creasing his wide brow.

"Anyone I know?"

"Probably. Grant Whitcomb."

Whitcomb's ranch bordered the reservation. He had an on-going feud with the reservation Indians, always accusing them of breaking down his fences, stealing his cattle and horses, and starting fires. Sometimes his accusations were justified, more often they were not.

"As much as he hates Indians, I can't imagine Mr. Whitcomb wanting anything to do with the Pow Wow," Tempe said.

"Obviously you don't know him very well, Deputy. He's a mean, vicious old man. He'd do anything to hurt me or my family." Jake's eyes narrowed and the crease deepened. He sighed, glancing all around once again. "If it was him, he's managed to find some place to hide. Might as well go back."

The dancers had left the circle and rejoined those waiting in line at the entrance to the arena by the time Tempe returned. The master-of-ceremonies once again stepped to the mike. "Everyone stand for the grand entry and remain standing for the entire ceremony."

At the head of the line were the elders. The men wore huge double bustles at their necks and backs, traditional dress, and red and black, double-feathered headdress.

With a slow, halting double step, the older people regally entered the arena first. The previous year's Princess followed, wearing a beautifully decorated shawl over a buckskin dress and a beaded crown perched atop a modern short hairdo.

The Princess hopefuls were in line behind her. They lifted their feet higher, swaying gracefully. Linda Davelos' spirits seemed to have risen with the beat of the drum. She held her head high; a smile brightened her plain face.

Some of the younger men hopped with a lively step, bowing and dipping in time with the rhythm as they entered the arena. One youth had cowbells circling his ankles, adding a discordant clanging to the drum beat and voice of the singer.

The children danced with as much exuberance as their older counterparts. A few of the young mothers carried their children on their backs in modern versions of the Indian backboard.

Some of the participants didn't look like Indians at all except for their clothing. Tempe decided they might be part Indian, but like Blair, it just didn't show.

All those dressed in regalia carried a feather of some sort--just one, or a fan of turkey, dyed chicken feathers, or a more spectacular spray of eagle feathers.

As Tempe watched, amazed by the differences in the outfits, she noticed one young man who stood out from the rest. He danced more exuberantly--and with less grace--passing the others. His dark shoulder length hair flowed freely from a headband with beading, ribbon streamers, and white beaded loops circling his black, deep-set eyes. Feathers covered his shoulders, leaving his torso bare. Low slung deerskin breeches covered muscular legs. His moccasins pounded against the sawdust as he moved past people, making his way towards the front of the line.

He appeared rude, or at least unmindful of those

around him, as he circled and dipped around one dancer, then another.

Though he continued to lift his knees high in perfect rhythm with the drum, he slipped in beside the Princess contestants.

The beaded loops cast a shadow on the young man's upper face, making him appear fierce and threatening. Tempe could imagine him as a warrior of long ago, preparing himself for battle.

Marella noticed him for the first time. She missed a beat of the rhythm, almost stumbling. Her mouth opened as though she was going to say something to him and she frowned. From the distance, Tempe couldn't be sure if her expression showed anger--or was it fear?

2

After all the Indians entered the arena and the royalty was introduced, an elder dressed in authentic regalia, including a double-feathered headdress, stepped forward to give the invocation. With one hand raised, he spoke in his native tongue.

"He's speaking to the Creator, Mother Earth, the four directions and the natural elements as well as to all the ancestors who walked here before us," Nick whispered. "It's a basic prayer thanking the Creator for providing the animals and all of nature for the People."

The prayer over, a color guard of Indians dressed in traditional costume brought the American and California flags to the front of the arena. The drums accompanying the singer began again. All of the songs were sung in native languages in the manner Indians had been singing for years.

"This is the flag song and it honors all of our veterans and warriors for protecting our country," Nick explained.

The ceremony ended and the drum beat continued as the people danced their way back out of the arena. As the Princess hopefuls made their way past Tempe, she noticed the young man with brooding good looks and the beaded loops circling his eyes continue to follow Marella Celso, though he stayed far enough away from her so she wouldn't notice him.

"What do you know about that one?" Tempe asked, as the youthful Indian ducked behind a booth selling T-shirts with the logo of the Pow Wow.

"He's like too many of our young men. Brash, has a chip on his shoulder. Drinking problem. A lot like I was at that age. His name is Daniel Redwing. Lives on the reservation," Nick said.

"What's his connection to Marella Celso?"

Nick grinned, showing his white teeth. "There isn't one...though he'd like there to be. Marella has a boyfriend, Cody Endrezza. You'll see him dancing today."

Someone came up to speak with Two John, and Tempe drifted away. The drum continued its consistent beat; another song had begun. It sounded much the same as the others. Tempe was aware more dancing had started.

As she walked around the outside of the bleachers she could see men, wearing feather bustles at their necks and backs, bowing and spinning and shaking their heads. Horsehair headdresses with one or two feathers on a rocker base moved in time to the beat of the drum. The fast dancing with its fluid body movements reminded Tempe of a war dance.

"Damnable savages!" a scratchy voice snarled behind her.

Tempe whirled around, immediately recognizing the cantankerous old rancher who trailed behind her. "Mr. Whitcomb." Jake had been right.

"Fine kettle of fish. Whose bright idea was it to let these horse thieves and cattle rustlers throw this big party, anyhow? Never heard of such daggone foolishness. Don't even make sense to let such a big bunch of 'em git together in one place." The wizened old man was several inches shorter than Tempe. He jammed his gnarled hands into the pockets of his faded, baggy overalls. His ever-present straw hat rested on his jutting ears, his liver-spotted wrinkled face looking even older than the sixty years Tempe knew him to be.

"If you don't approve, Mr. Whitcomb, why on earth did you come?" Tempe asked.

"Wanted to see for myself what this buffoonery was all about." The old man screwed his face into a sneer that reflected his distaste.

"Now that you've seen it, maybe you ought to leave," Tempe suggested. She'd noticed some of the Indian youth had heard Whitcomb's deprecating remarks and glared at him menacingly.

"I got just as much right to be here as anyone else.

I paid my entrance fee. See!" He held up the back of his hand to show her the stamp that everyone received on entering.

"If you're determined to stay, watch how you talk, okay?" Tempe knew he wouldn't heed her words.

"This is a free country! I got a right to my opinions just like the next guy." Whitcomb lifted his hat and swiped at his thinning but still sandy-colored hair.

Tempe spotted a suspicious bulge in one of the many pockets of his overalls. It looked to be the shape of a gun. "What's that you have there?" Tempe pointed.

"None of your damn business, Deputy" Whitcomb started to move away from her.

"Wait a minute, Mr. Whitcomb, I'm not through talking to you."

"Well, I'm through talking to you," and he loped away with a slight limp.

It wasn't worth going after him, she couldn't search him without a reason. She knew Whitcomb owned many guns, had permits for them all. If it were a gun in his pocket, she hoped he had sense enough to keep it there. She'd have to watch him.

"What's that old fool doing here?" Violet Celso appeared beside Tempe.

"That's just what I was asking him," Tempe said, watching Whitcomb until he disappeared around the corner of one of the booths.

"I hate to see him, he's nothing but trouble. I hope

he doesn't cross my husband's path. There's terrible bad blood between Jake and Mr. Whitcomb."

"Jake told me. But from what I've heard, there's bad blood between Whitcomb and all the reservation Indians," Tempe said.

"True. But Jake's and Mr. Whitcomb's feuding goes way back. Every time something happened to one of Mr. Whitcomb's animals he always came looking for Jake. He has it in his head that Jake is always to blame, no matter what."

"I've heard that he's accused plenty of the younger Indians of various crimes also." Hardly a week went by that Mr. Whitcomb didn't make a complaint against one Indian or another for a variety of transgressions ranging from illegal burning to trespassing.

"He's unhappy if he sees them breathing," Violet said.

"He just doesn't like us, that's why it seems so crazy for him to be here. I hope he isn't up to something."

"Surely he wouldn't start any trouble--he's certainly outnumbered."

"The man is crazy, Deputy Crabtree. I wouldn't put anything past him. Frankly, it makes me nervous. He absolutely hates my family...we try to stay out of his path." Violet's round face showed her concern.

Tempe put her hand on the shorter woman's shoulder. "Don't worry, I'll watch out for him. By the way, I saw your daughter during the ceremonial. She's absolutely gorgeous."

Violet smiled. "Thank you. And she's as nice as she is beautiful. Jake and I are certainly proud of her. She'll make a wonderful Princess."

"You sound positive she'll get it."

Nodding, the proud mother said, "She'd already sold more tickets than any of the other girls before the day started. No one ever turns her down."

Tempe again became aware of the insistent drum beat. "That drumming kind of gets to me."

Violet chuckled. "It's supposed to. We're to become one with the drum. Your heart should start beating in rhythm with it."

"I wish I understood the significance of everything."

"Don't worry about it. Many Indians don't. I think I better go now, and let Jake know he was right about Mr. Whitcomb being here." Violet started toward the arena, and Tempe watched her walk away. From the back, except for her curly hair, Violet looked like a squaw from the past, with her fringed buckskin dress and moccasins.

Tempe began a circle around the arena, watching for Grant Whitcomb. She hoped the old man would soon get bored and head back to his ranch.

She didn't spot the rancher but did see the four Princess contestants busily peddling their tickets. Katherine Davelos dogged the steps of her daughter, at times actually shoving the girl toward new arrivals.

After circling the arena twice and patrolling through the area where the Indian merchandise and Pow Wow souvenirs were being sold, Tempe headed toward the entrance. She strolled past the food booths, amused by the long line for buffalo burgers.

Looking over the picnic tables, she smiled at the families enjoying their burgers, Indian tacos, and sodas. The crowd seemed happy and content to be part of the Native American celebration. She didn't see Grant Whitcomb anywhere; maybe he'd taken her advice after all and headed home.

The square cement building that housed the restrooms was on the far side of the entrance. Beyond it was a fence surrounding the area where the carnival rides were erected during the fair, as well as the building which housed exhibits, but neither were in use for the Pow Wow. Though the bathroom was popular, there was no reason for anyone to venture much beyond it.

The singing stopped and started but it seemed like the drum never ceased. The constant beat trailed Tempe.

When she returned to the arena area, she spotted a TV crew. Tempe watched them interview the older couple who had led the processional.

When they finished, Katherine Davelos yanked her daughter by the arm, pushing her in front of the camera. "Tell them about yourself, Linda."

Obviously embarrassed, the girl bit her lip, hanging her head so her hair hid her face.

"Stand up straight!" Katherine ordered. "Smile."

The television newscaster, a tall black man, must have felt compassion for the girl. "Yes, do give us a smile. And tell us your name."

"Linda Davelos." Her full lower lip quivered, and she looked as though all she wanted to do was escape.

"And I understand you're one of the contestants for the Princess contest."

"Yes, sir."

"And is that one of your fellow contestants?" the man asked, stepping over to Marella who'd just sold several tickets to a young couple with a baby.

"Yes, sir."

The cameraman focused on Marella. When she noticed him she smiled, her dark eyes sparkling.

"Hi, I'm Marella Celso."

"Will you tell us a little about yourself, Marella, and why you'd like to be the Princess of this Pow Wow?" the newsman asked.

Marella looked and acted like a Princess. She held her head proudly as she spoke, her hip length hair shining. Her golden skin glowed. "I'm seventeen and a senior at Dennison High School. Being the Princess of the Pow Wow is something I've wanted to do ever since I attended my first Pow Wow. I'm proud of my Yanduchi heritage, and as the Princess, I will have the opportunity to represent my people."

"Thank you, Marella," the newsman said, before

taking off to find someone else to interview.

"You always have to butt in, don't you, Marella. Couldn't you see he was interviewing Linda?" Katherine snapped.

Marella shrugged, turning her back on the woman, her long hair swinging around her body. Katherine looked after her, her tanned face distorted with hatred.

3

Though the drumming continued, Tempe noticed it less and less. As Violet had suggested, it almost became a part of her though she wasn't sure if her own heart actually kept time with the drum.

The crowd continued to be well-mannered, obviously enthralled by the dancing, pleased with the food and souvenir offerings. Tempe had little to do except circulate through the grounds and watch the various dances herself. She took time out to eat a bowl of buffalo meat chili, which she found spicy and delicious.

Noticing a large gathering around a double booth, Tempe strode over to see what had attracted them. It was a demonstration of Indian crafts. A pony-tailed man in his early thirties worked on a soapstone carving with several examples of his finished product displayed on the table before him.

Two older women, one thin and one heavy, both gray-haired with brown, weathered skin, sat side-by-side. The thin one wore a denim fringed shirt and faded jeans, her long fingers moving swiftly as she wove thin willow shoots into a basket.

The other woman strung blue, green, amber, white, ruby red, and lavender beads on milkweed fibers, fashioning them into intricate designs.

"What is that you're using to make the baskets?" a bespectacled woman asked.

Without looking up, the weaver said, "This is willow. For a water-tight basket you must have white root from sage. The black root and red bud is used for the design. Sourberry bushes have the longest and straightest roots."

As more questions were asked and answered, another, more intense conversation going on nearby caught Tempe's attention. Several feet behind the booth, near the vine-covered fence that surrounded the fair grounds, Marella Celso stood talking to a tall young man dressed in buckskin regalia decorated with feathers. His face had been painted with streaks of black, red, yellow and white, making him appear ferocious. But his gestures and stance seemed plaintive, almost begging.

Marella had her arms crossed over the rainbow colored beading on the white bodice of her dress. The endearing smile that had helped her sell so many tickets was gone as she fixed her black eyes upon the young man.

Tempe eased her way around the side of the booth to be closer to the couple.

"...you've got to change your mind, Marella. I love you, don't you know that?"

"You're wasting your time, Cody. I explained everything to you last night. I've made my decision." Marella spun away, her long, mahogany hair swirling around her body.

Cody clamped his hand on her shoulder, halting her progress. "I'm not going to accept your decision. You've got to listen to me!"

Putting her own hand over his, Marella moved it away. Without turning around, she lifted her chin and spoke quietly. "Isn't it time for your dance?" With her chin still held high, she walked away from him.

"I don't care about the dancing, Marella. All I care about is you," Cody called after her.

Marella didn't turn around.

Cody stamped his mocassined foot. He sighed, and strode toward the arena. Tempe followed him.

A group of men dressed similarly to Cody were receiving a smoke blessing from Violet. When she spotted the young man, her round face brightened. "There you are! I thought you weren't going to make it!"

She waved the smoke in his direction.

The announcer's voice came over the loud speaker. "Now we have the men's Northern Traditional."

A singer began and the leather clad, feather decorated men danced into the arena. The foot and body movements seemed unique to each dancer. It appeared as though Cody had forgotten his encounter with Marella, as he bobbed and gyrated in time with the drum beat.

Violet stood beside Tempe as they watched. She pointed toward Cody, and with pride in her voice said, "That's Cody Endrezza, Marella's boy friend. I suspect there are wedding bells in the future for them."

Tempe didn't say anything about the confrontation she'd witnessed between the young couple though she couldn't help but wonder what it meant as far as their relationship was concerned. "Tell me about this dance, Violet."

"It represents the spirit of battles and hunts. Each one dances as he feels, perhaps using the movements of the bear, the wolf, the eagle or the hawk." Violet gazed into the arena, her eyes following her daughter's suitor. "Cody is one of the head dancers, that's why he's so perfect for Marella. I know he'll always conduct himself in a manner reflecting the dignity and exemplary conduct of a traditional dancer."

Tempe hoped that would be true as he worked his way through the disagreement he had with Marella. But young love was often fraught with disagreement. If the relationship was meant to be, they would surely solve their problem.

A commotion in one of the grandstands captured Tempe's attention. Tempe recognized Linda Davelo's green satin gown as she jogged past a row of the startled audience. As she drew nearer, Tempe could see the girl was crying.

Her mother came after her, waving a book of tickets in one hand, a handful of dollar bills in the other. "Linda, come back here right now! How do you expect to win if you don't sell your tickets? I was just trying to help. Don't be so silly, Linda."

Holding her skirt, Linda dashed down the bleacher stairs and jumped off the end. She ran around the corner and disappeared. Katherine followed, unable to keep up because of her high-heeled boots.

When she noticed Tempe and Violet watching, she paused long enough to snarl, "What're you looking at? Don't think it's over, Violet Celso! My Linda is going to be the Princess!"

"That woman!" Violet shook her head. "I'm convinced there's some good in everyone, but it's certainly difficult to find any in Katherine."

They turned their attention back to the arena just as Cody maneuvered in a particularly exuberant manner. One of the feathers adorning his costume came loose, fluttering to the ground.

"Oh no!" Violet gasped.

"What's the matter?"

"An eagle feather isn't supposed to touch the ground. Cody will be upset."

The young man continued dancing, but he and all the others were careful not to step on the fallen feather. Tempe wondered why Cody didn't pick it up. But within a few minutes, an older man came from the sidelines and carefully retrieved the feather.

"Only a veteran can do that," Violet explained.

Tempe remained with Violet until the dance ended. Each of the dancers stopped exactly with the last drum beat. As the others filed out of the arena, Cody approached the veteran with his hand outstretched.

The two men shook hands and Cody gave him some money. Tempe looked to Violet for an explanation. "That's part of the tradition."

There was so much more to this Indian business than Tempe had ever imagined.

As she resumed her circling of the arena, Tempe spotted the other two Princess contestants laughing and talking with two young men, one dressed in a Native American outfit and the other in Levis and T-shirt.

Further on, she passed Marella, obviously recovered from her encounter with Cody, as she smiled brightly at two older couples who were purchasing tickets from her. Looking past them, Tempe noticed Daniel Redwing standing with a large group of Indian youths. Like Daniel, most of them wore native clothing. But while the other young men conversed with each other, Daniel focused on Marella.

Tempe wished she could see the expression in Redwing's eyes, but the beaded loops of his headband completely shaded them.

When Marella moved away from the couples, searching for potential customers, Daniel Redwing broke away from his companions. Though he didn't follow Marella's path exactly, Redwing darted from one place to another, almost as though he was stalking the girl.

Deciding she ought to let him know she was mindful of what he was doing, Tempe quickened her step in order to catch up with Redwing. Before she could reach him, she heard shouting and sounds of a scuffle back at the arena area.

Spinning on her heel, she broke into a run. Nick Two John held a struggling Jake Celso, while Abel Contreras pinned a kicking and screaming Grant Whitcomb against the wall of the grandstand.

"Lemme go, you stinkin' redskin!" Whitcomb yelled, spitting at Contreras. His straw hat fell to the ground.

"Come on, Two John, let loose. That old man needs to be thrown out on his butt," Jake said.

"What's going on here?" Tempe asked.

"That old man keeps bad mouthing Indians," Jake said. "He doesn't belong here."

"I got just as much right to be here as any of them," Whitcomb growled, but he'd stopped his kicking.

"I spoke to you about that once before, Mr. Whitcomb. I think you'd better be going," Tempe said.

"I ain't leaving, and you can't make me," Whitcomb said. "You're no better than the rest of these half-breeds, Deputy. There ain't no law saying I can't be here."

There was a time when being called a half-breed

would have angered Tempe, but no longer. As a deputy, she'd been called so many bad names, none of them bothered her. "If you keep causing trouble, I'll have to arrest you. Wouldn't it just be easier for you to go home?"

Whitcomb lifted his pointy chin, stretching his wrinkled wattle. "I paid good money to see what this Injun hoopla is all about, and I'm staying."

Tempe looked at his pocket where she'd spotted the bulge that looked like a gun and was gratified to see it no longer there. At least he must have had some common sense about that and locked it up in his vehicle.

Nick released Celso and pulled some bills from inside his vest. "Here, Mr. Whitcomb. Take this, it's what you paid to get in here and more."

The old man stepped back, holding up his hands. "I don't want your money, Two John."

Jake put his nose next to Whitcomb's. "Get your skinny ass out of here now before I forget you're an old man."

Reaching out and grabbing his arm, Contreras pulled Celso back. "Hey, cool down, Jake, we're supposed to be keeping order here."

With his hands balled into fists, Jake turned his back on Whitcomb, his clenched jaw quivering. "The man makes me so mad I forget everything."

"I don't know what he's got to be mad about," Whitcomb whined as he retrieved his hat and stuck in on his head. "I'm the one he's been stealing from all these years."

"Take him away, Deputy," Nick said. "I don't know how long we'll be able to control Jake."

Linking her arm with the old man, Tempe said, "Come on, Mr. Whitcomb, you and I need to talk."

"There's nothing for us to talk about, woman. Of course you're gonna side with them damned Injuns, you got that same kind of lying, cheating blood in your veins." Whitcomb almost had to run to keep up with Tempe's long-legged stride as she dragged him along beside her.

He protested and bad-mouthed her all the way. She took him to the far side of the building that housed the restrooms so that no one could hear them.

"What 'cha gonna do now? Beat me up?" That the old man actually feared she might do just that was apparent in the way he cringed away from her.

"Of course I'm not going to beat you up, but we are going to come to an understanding. If you won't leave, Mr. Whitcomb, then you have to promise to behave."

Quickly regaining his composure, Whitcomb stretched his wrinkled neck, pulling himself up until he stood nearly as tall as Tempe. "I don't know what you mean."

"I'll explain it to you very carefully. You can think all the bad thoughts you want to about Indians or any- one else, but while you're on these premises, I don't want you making one more nasty crack. Do you hear me?"

"I hear you," he growled.

"I mean it, Mr. Whitcomb. If one more person complains to me about you, I'm calling for back-up and you will be arrested and go to jail. Have you got that?"

"You can't arrest me for calling people bad names," he said, but he looked as though he wasn't sure.

"I can if I decide you are disturbing the peace," Tempe said. "And there's something else."

"What's that?"

"I know all about the feud you've got going with the Celso family, but you're going to forget it for as long as you're here at this Pow Wow. Understand?"

"But you don't know what them and their like been doing to me over the years...."

"I don't care about any of that. For today you'll stay far away from Jake and Violet Celso and their daughter. Have you got that?"

"There ain't no way you can...."

With her fists on her hips, Tempe stared at him using her most intimidating expression. "Mr. Whitcomb, I am the law here. You will do as I say, or you are out of here!"

"Yes, ma'am!" The old rancher skittered away from Tempe, looking back over his shoulder several times.

"My, my, sweetheart, so that's how you put the

fear of God into the crooks. I wondered how my beautiful bride upheld the law--now I know." Hutch kissed her on the cheek.

Because she'd been concentrating on Whitcomb, she hadn't noticed her husband approaching. Laughing, she cradled his face with her hands and kissed him on the lips. "Am I happy to see you!"

"Thank you! I finished writing my sermon and thought if we were going to spend any time together this weekend I'd better come to the Pow Wow."

"Good thinking."

Holding hands, they strolled past the cement building toward the refreshment stands and the arena beyond. A few people stared, no doubt surprised to see a uniformed deputy being so chummy with a civilian. But it might be Hutch's thatch of auburn hair and freckled skin that attracted the attention.

"What was going on between you and that old man? You looked positively ready to eat him alive."

"That's Grant Whitcomb. He owns a ranch right next to the reservation. There's been bad blood between him and the Indians forever. He's been making derogatory remarks about them ever since he arrived."

"If he doesn't like Indians, why on earth did he come here?" Hutch adjusted his glasses as he looked around at the milling crowd which consisted mostly of Indians.

"That's a good question. But I think it's just because he's such an ornery old coot, he enjoys being troublesome. Have you had anything to eat? I ate some buffalo chili, and it was pretty good."

"I had a sandwich at home. Maybe I'll try something later."

"What's Blair up to?"

Hutch laughed. "Do you really have to ask? He's at the fire station, as usual." Though not quite old enough to officially serve as a volunteer fireman, Blair had taken all the training and the Chief let him go on calls. After he graduated from high school, he planned to go on to college and major in fire science. "What do you think about the Pow Wow?"

"It's quite a production. Did you know Nick Two John organized it?"

"Nope, had no idea. Is he around, I'd like to say hello to him."

"We'll go over to the arena so you can see some of the dances. Nick can explain the significance of everything to you. There's far more to all this than I ever imagined. It's truly impressive."

"You weren't looking forward to being here this morning. Sounds as though you've changed your mind. That's good." Hutch smiled down at her, showing his dimpled cheek.

"I thought it would be boring," Tempe said. "I can assure you, it hasn't been. Besides Grant Whitcomb, there are several other intriguing personalities around."

"Anyone I know?"

"I doubt it, since they're from the reservation. One of the young women who is running for Princess has two fellows chasing after her. I don't think she's happy with either one of them at the moment...though her mother feels certain one is going to be her daughter's future husband.

"And then there's the mother of another of the Princess contestants who is determined her daughter will win."

"Sounds like a plot for a soap opera. You'll have to point all these people out to me." Hutch laughed.

With her husband by her side, the remainder of the afternoon promised to be most pleasant. Having Hutch join her made the episode with Grant Whitcomb seem almost humorous, erasing any real threat to the peacefulness of the Pow Wow. Katherine Davelos' hatred for Violet Celso seemed petty, while the pursuit of Marella by Cody Endrezza and Daniel Redwing indicated nothing other than adolescent behavior. None of it cause for concern, she decided.

4

After greeting Hutch warmly, Nick Two John proudly launched into his explanation in answer to Hutch's question about the event ending with, "Traditionally a Pow Wow was held during the summer when game was plentiful. Tribes came together for the buffalo hunt."

The master-of-ceremonies stepped to the microphone. "The Round dance is next. Everyone may participate."

Many flowed into the arena, men and women, teenagers, little children, some wearing Indian outfits and some not.

Holding his hand out to Tempe, Nick said, "Come, this is a dance you can be a part of."

She leaned against Hutch and laughingly shook her head. "I don't think so."

Hutch grasped her shoulders, "Go ahead, Tempe. You'll enjoy it."

It wasn't so very long ago that Hutch had shown

signs of jealousy toward Two John. Encouraging her to dance with him surely meant all traces of the emotion had disappeared. She was glad her husband had conquered his unwarranted feelings, but she wasn't thrilled about making a fool of herself.

"I have no idea what to do," she said, pulling away from Nick as he grasped her hand.

"It's easy. Just follow everyone else." He led her to the large circle that had been formed. A girl of about twelve smiled at her and clasped her other hand.

The drum began. And the large group started moving, everyone lifting their feet in time to the beat. It didn't take long for Tempe to figure out how to do the simplest of the steps while swaying her body. At first, she worried about how strange it must look for a uniformed deputy sheriff to be joining in the dancing. Two steps on one foot, two on the other, always keeping time with the drum. Advancing in the circle as one with all the rest. She no longer thought of anything else but the hypnotic beat.

When it was over, Two John nodded to her. "Now we are all brothers and sisters."

"That was great! Thank you Nick."

Hutch welcomed her with open arms and a kiss. "You looked just like you've been doing that all your life."

"I can't believe how exhilarating it was!"

The master-of-ceremonies announced the next dance. Several groups of young boys, their regalia decorated with fringes and ribbons scurried past them into the arena. "You can stay here and watch, Hutch," Tempe said. "But it's time I earned my salary and took another look around."

"I'd rather come with you," Hutch said. "Thanks for taking the time to explain everything, Nick."

"My pleasure." The handsome Indian had already turned his attention to the dance, the ribbons and fringes on the boy's outfits rippling as they moved to the rhythm of the drum.

Tempe and Hutch slowly walked from one end of the grounds to the other. Hutch paused at each booth to examine the wares, while Tempe searched faces, looking for potential problems. The crowd continued to swell as the day wore on towards evening, but everyone seemed to be having a good time--everyone except Grant Whitcomb.

They paused to talk to the old man as he sat at a picnic table eating a buffalo burger. Tempe introduced him to her husband.

"How's the burger?" Hutch asked. "I've been thinking about trying one of those."

"It's edible...that's about all I can say for it," Whitcomb grumbled, shoving his hat further back on his head.

"I'm going to have one anyway...yours looks mighty tempting. Do you want anything, sweetheart?"

"A soda would be fine."

Since Whitcomb had been her only problem so far,

Tempe sat down across from him. Maybe she could talk him into going home. "Have you seen anything of interest yet, Mr. Whitcomb?"

"You made me promise not to say anything bad so I can't tell you what I think." Whitcomb glared at her.

"Surely there must be something that you approve of."

"Not a daggone thing, Deputy. It's a big waste of time and money to my way of thinking."

"If you're so miserable, why don't you go home? I don't understand why you keep hanging around here when you dislike everything that's going on."

The old man sat straighter. "No way. That's what you all want, and I ain't about to give it to you." He wrapped up what was left of his burger and threw it into the trash can at the end of the table.

He winced as he lifted his leg over the bench and stood up.

"Okay, Mr. Whitcomb. Just remember what I told you before. No bad-mouthing anyone, or you're going to jail."

"I heard you the first time, Deputy." Whitcomb hobbled away from her, quickly disappearing into the crowd.

"Drove him away again, did you?" Hutch said, as he slid in beside her.

"Wish I could drive him home," Tempe said. "The old guy has made himself so miserable with hatred, I don't think he could have a good time if he tried."

"Deputy Crabtree!" Abel Contreras came running toward her. "We got trouble at the arena."

"Sorry, Hutch." Tempe jumped up from the bench.

"Don't worry about me, I'll just be here enjoying my buffalo burger."

She dashed after Contreras, excusing herself as they darted in and out of the moving groups of people. She wondered what kind of trouble Abel was leading her into.

Jake held a wriggling Daniel Redwing. The young man swung his head causing the ribbon streamers on his headband to whip back and forth. "It isn't true. You just don't want me to dance with Marella!"

Marella stood off to the side, watching the scene with obvious distaste.

"I think the situation is that my daughter doesn't want to dance with you, Redwing," Jake said, not releasing his hold.

"It doesn't really matter," Two John interjected. "You know the rules about drinking."

Redwing quit thrashing about, but leaned away from Jake. "What makes you think I had anything to drink?"

"Ha! Your breath reeks of alcohol," Jake said. "Will you please escort him off the fairgrounds, Deputy?"

"Come along, Redwing," Tempe said. Jake shoved Daniel toward her. She grasped the young man's upper arm and began leading him through the crowd.

Katherine Davelos and her daughter, Linda, had been among the many watching the spectacle. Katherine shook a long-nailed finger in Linda's face. "Disgusting, absolutely disgusting. What kind of a girl must Marella be to attract such rubbish?"

That woman's attitude was getting worse. If Tempe didn't already have her hands full escorting Redwing from the premises, she'd have taken the time to talk to Katherine. In her own way she was becoming as much of a problem as Whitcomb.

But Tempe did have her hands full. Though Redwing didn't try to get away from her, she had to push him through the crowd. When she neared the entrance, Hutch joined her.

"What's this?" he murmured.

"At the request of Pow Wow security, I'm helping Mr. Redwing off the premises," Tempe explained.

Hutch walked alongside her as she led the sullen Indian toward the exit gate. "What'd he do?"

"He's been drinking. There's no liquor allowed at the Pow Wow."

Redwing pulled up short. "I didn't bring any liquor into the Pow Wow."

Tempe stared past the beaded loops into Redwing's deep set eyes. "Which means you've got some out in your vehicle. For your sake, you better keep your mouth shut. You don't want to end up in jail."

Yanking his arm out of Tempe's grasp, Redwing spun on his moccasined feet and pushed his way through the exit turnstile.

"If looks could kill you'd be in terrible shape," Hutch said.

"If looks could kill I wouldn't be here today." Tempe laughed. "Fielding dirty looks is part of my job. Come on, let's go back and see what's going on in the arena now."

Tempe and Hutch watched more dances, listened to Nick Two John's explanations about the significance of each one, and circled the arena again. Periodically, Tempe spotted Grant Whitcomb skulking around, but he didn't seem to be bothering anyone. And the Princess contestants continued to sell their tickets.

Evening came with even more Pow Wow enthusiasts. The grandstands were packed, the level of anticipation raised, as everyone awaited the coronation.

Tempe tucked her arm through the crook of Hutch's elbow. "Let's head back to the arena. I want to see who's going to win this big event."

As they walked along with the crowd, mostly Indians, Hutch said, "I'm just amazed at the number of Native Americans."

"Some of them don't look much like Indians," Tempe observed. "Isn't it interesting how times change? When I was a teenager I was ashamed of my mixed blood. Today everyone is proud to have even the tiniest bit of Indian ancestry."

"That's certainly better, isn't it?"

When they neared the arena, Violet Celso came

running up to Tempe. Worry furrowed her wide fore-head. "Have you seen Marella? The other girls are lined up and ready to go."

"Not for a while," Tempe said.

Linda and the other two contestants stood by the tables near the grandstands. Surprisingly, Katherine Davelos was nowhere in sight. It was the first time Tempe had seen Linda without her mother. Some-thing very urgent must have come up for Katherine to leave her daughter alone when it was so near to the time for the winning Princess to be named.

"What about Cody Endrezza? No one seems to know where he is either." Violet looked past Tempe and Hutch, eyes busily searching the crowd.

"Tempe, didn't you tell me those two are sweet-hearts?" Hutch asked. "Maybe they went off some-place and just lost track of the time."

It was possible, of course. Perhaps they were in the process of making up from their earlier disagree-ment.

Violet shook her curly head. "Marella knows the schedule. She's so conscientious and this contest means so much to her, I can't imagine anything caus-ing her to forget what time it is. She hasn't even turned in all of her ticket money."

That was cause for distress. Tempe had noticed the rolls of bills the girls were carrying around with them. "Don't worry, Mrs. Celso, I'll look for her."

"I've already been through the booths. She isn't

around there," Violet pointed out.

Though she and Hutch had just come from the other side and hadn't noticed Marella, Tempe said, "I'll head back the other way. Maybe she's in the bathroom combing her hair and putting on fresh lipstick."

Violet's mouth lifted in a smile, but her eyes didn't look as though she believed Tempe's suggestion. "I bet you're right. Probably brushing her hair. She always has to brush her hair."

"When I find her, I'll hurry her along," Tempe said.

"I'll go with you," Hutch said. Violet acted as though she would like to join them, but Tempe took off without asking her.

Before they reached the square block building which housed the restrooms, Katherine Davelos rushed past them, heading in the direction of the arena. Tempe tried to hail her, "Mrs. Davelos, have you seen...."

The woman acted as though she hadn't heard.

"What's the matter with her?" Hutch asked. "She looks upset about something."

"I don't think she is ever happy." At the open door to the women's half of the building, Tempe paused. "I'll be right out."

Inside, there was a line for the stalls. Four teen-aged girls stood at the mirror, three combed their hair while one put on mascara. No Marella. She looked at the feet under the doors, but none wore white moccasins.

To be sure, she said loudly, "Marella! Marella

Celso, are you in here?"

Everyone turned to look at her curiously. "I'm looking for Marella Celso, has anyone seen her?"

Heads shook and shoulders shrugged. Tempe stepped back outside. "She's not there."

Hutch said. "Where now?"

"The only place we haven't been is the other side of that fence. I can't imagine any reason for Marella to be over there, but we better look just in case."

Tempe led the way. The lights weren't on so she took her flashlight off her utility belt and flipped it on.

Following the bright beam, they came to the gate. It stood ajar. "I'm sure this was closed earlier today." She began to feel uneasy.

Tempe swept the flashlight beam from side to side to examine the area. On one side was the vast empty space reserved for carnival rides, to the right was the large exhibit building. Tempe led the way as she and Hutch rounded the corner of the building.

The flashlight beam fell upon what looked like a pile of white rags. "Oh, oh, what's that?"

Trotting, Tempe headed toward the rags. It didn't take long for her to see that it was a body.

Long, mahogany hair fanned out around the colorfully beaded bodice of the white, fringed Indian gown.

"We've found Marella."

5

What's wrong with her?" Hutch asked.

Tempe knelt beside the girl's body. Long wisps of hair fell across the face but didn't cover the small, dark hole in her temple.

Though positive Marella was dead, Tempe knelt beside her and pressed her fingers against the carotid artery searching for a pulse. There was none, though the flesh was still warm. "She's dead." Tempe glanced at her watch and noted the time. Nearly seven.

Hutch took a step nearer.

"Don't come any closer," she warned, standing up. Marella's right arm had been flung away, inches from her hand was a Colt "45 revolver. Tempe pointed the flashlight toward it.

"Dear God, did the girl kill herself?"

"Girls seldom shoot themselves on purpose." Tempe turned on her portable radio. "While I make the report, I'd like you to go to the entrance and wait for the deputies. Let them know where I am. But don't tell anyone else what we've found."

"I hate to leave you here by yourself," Hutch said.

She waved him off. Though her husband looked back once, he quickly disappeared around the corner of the building while she radioed the dispatcher about the murder.

While waiting for help, Tempe continued to move the flashlight around in an effort to spot clues without contaminating the crime scene. She knew the saw-dust covering the ground had prevented any footprints but there might be something else.

At first glance, the fact that the gun was close to Marella did suggest suicide but she hadn't appeared the least bit depressed. There didn't seem to be any powder flash burns or tattoo marks on the flesh around the bullet hole; those would have been there if she'd shot herself.

Tempe was sure the girl had been murdered, but who could have done it?

As she continued the sweep with the flashlight, she heard the sound of approaching sirens. Several feet away from the gun, Tempe spotted a single feather. She'd have to move closer to be sure, but it looked like an eagle feather.

Cody Endrezza lost one of his eagle feathers while dancing. Maybe he reattached it and it came loose again. Perhaps Marella's and Cody's disagreement had escalated to such a degree he'd killed her. Or the mur-derer had planted the feather to cast suspicion on Cody.

Then there was always Katherine Davelos. She'd been coming from this general direction just minutes before Tempe discovered the body. Could she really have been desperate enough to have her own daughter win the Princess contest that she'd kill the greatest competitor?

It would be important to find out who the gun belonged to, but why would the murderer leave it behind? Just like the eagle feather, the gun could be another plant. Maybe the murderer thought he or she had made it look enough like suicide that no further investigation would be done.

The shrill cry of sirens filled the night as they neared the fairgrounds. Tempe knew it wouldn't be long before the news of Marella Celso's death would have to be broken to her parents.

Bradley, a young and smoothly handsome deputy, arrived first. "Hey, Crabtree." He stepped close enough to view the body but not disturb the scene. "The detectives and the coroner are on the way."

"How about standing guard at the gate? Once folks realize what's going on there'll likely be a stampede."

Firemen arrived next, carrying emergency medical equipment. After a quick examination, the captain agreed with Tempe that Marella was beyond help. More deputies appeared as well as an ambulance crew. Tempe reminded everyone to keep their distance in order to preserve the crime scene. Nothing more could be done until the detectives arrived.

Detectives Richards and Morrison, wearing suits as usual, rounded the corner. Tall and lean, Richards squinted at her. "Out of your territory, aren't you, Crabtree?"

"Not really. I'm on special assignment for the Pow Wow," Tempe explained.

Morrison squatted beside the body. "Did you I.D. the victim?"

Talking to Morrison's broad back, Tempe said, "Her name is Marella Celso."

The huge man stood and turned around. "Are you the one who found the body?"

Tempe nodded. "Marella was one of the contestants for Pow Wow Princess. When it was time for the winner to be announced, Marella couldn't be found. Her mother asked me to look for her."

Richards said, "Does the mother know?"

"No. Both of her parents are here."

"Rough," Morrison grunted.

"Anybody around when you found the body?" Richards asked.

Again Tempe shook her head.

"What're the chances the kid did herself in?"

"I didn't really know Marella but what I saw of her today makes me think she wouldn't commit suicide. Besides being beautiful, she was popular and most likely would have been crowned Princess this evening."

"What about boyfriends? Girls do stupid things

over broken hearts," Morrison said. Talk of broken hearts seemed incongruous coming from the linebacker-sized man with the lopsided nose on his ugly face.

"She did have a verbal confrontation with the young man who is supposed to be her boyfriend earlier today. Cody Endrezza."

"Find this Endrezza, we'll want to talk to him," Richards said.

"What about the parents? Do you want me to break the news to them?"

"Yeah," Morrison growled, "suppose you'll have to. We'll want to talk to them as soon as we're through here. But it would be best if the Pow Wow could continue like nothing happened."

"I'll talk to the man in charge," Tempe said. There was more that she ought to tell the detectives but it would have to wait.

The Celsos stood anxiously just outside the fence, along with Hutch and a small gathering of the curious. Fortunately, the majority of those attending the Pow Wow had remained in the arena area. When Marella's parents spied Tempe coming toward them, Violet broke away from her husband.

"Deputy Crabtree, did you find Marella?"

Jake caught up to his wife and put his arm around her. "It's bad news, isn't it? Something's wrong with my baby."

Tempe took hold of Violet's hand. Hutch joined

them.

"Yes, I'm afraid it's very bad news. Marella is dead. I'm so sorry."

Violet screamed and sagged against her husband, her hand tightening around Tempe's.

"Tell me exactly what happened," Jake said, his eyes narrowing.

"We don't know what happened...just that she's been shot."

"Shot?" Jake looked as though he didn't believe Tempe.

Tempe nodded.

"Who did it?" He frowned fiercely. Even if Tempe had known she wouldn't have told him; he looked ready to commit murder himself.

"We don't know that either," Tempe said.

Through her tears, Violet said, "I want to see her."

"I'm afraid you can't just yet. The detectives do want to talk to you, but it will be a while," Tempe said.

"Maybe I can help," Hutch interjected. "Why don't we go over to those tables and sit down? Tempe can tell the deputies where you'll be."

Jake started to protest but Violet began sobbing hysterically. He pulled her closer and Hutch led them away. Tempe told Deputy Bradley to let the detectives know where the Celsos were before she hurried toward the arena.

Even though the crowning of the Princess had been

next on the schedule, Nick must have improvised since Tempe could hear the drum, and caught glimpses of dancers in colorful outfits moving around the arena. When she reached the entrance, Two John and Contreras hurried toward her.

Keeping his voice low, Nick asked, "What's all the excitement? Where are the Celsos?"

"Marella's dead," Tempe said.

Both men's expressions revealed the shock they felt from her news. "What happened to her?" Nick asked.

"Do Jake and Violet know?" Abel asked.

"Yes. Marella was shot."

"Oh, my God!" Nick exclaimed. "Who did it?"

"We don't know yet. But, Nick, the detectives in charge want you to continue with the Pow Wow."

"But we can't present the Princess...Marella won. None of the others even came close," Two John said.

"You'll have to do something," Abel said. "That's why there's so many people here tonight. They all want to know who won."

Two John lowered his head, remaining quiet for several moments. When he finally looked at Tempe again, he said, "We'll announce that due to unfortunate circumstances Marella had to drop out of the race. The second in line will be crowned Princess. Does that meet with your approval, Crabtree?"

"Sounds good."

Katherine pushed her way between Tempe and Two

John. With her fists on her hips and her legs spread apart, she pushed her nose within inches of Nick's. "I demand to know what's going on. Why haven't you begun the crowning of the Princess? If you're just holding off because Marella isn't here, she should be disqualified. All the contestants knew what time to be here."

"Exactly right, Mrs. Davelos. Since Mrs. Celso isn't here, why don't you get the girls into position."

Katherine appeared startled by Nick's quick agreement. "Well...of course...I'll be glad to."

Tempe noticed that Katherine moved Linda in front of the other two girls despite her daughter's unmistakable reluctance.

The drum stopped and the dancers filed out. Nick Two John stepped onto the grandstand and murmured an explanation to the puzzled looking master-of-ceremonies, before stepping up to the mike.

"Ladies and gentlemen, may I have your attention please. We've had a change in our plans for the evening. One of the contestants for Princess has been forced to drop out of the running."

A low murmur ran through the audience.

"At this time we would like to present the remaining contestants to you." Nick signaled to the girls to enter the arena.

No drum beat accompanied their approach which Tempe found surprising. She decided the unexpected announcement had taken the men at the drums by surprise.

"I will introduce each of the contestants before announcing the winner of our Princess contest. The first one is Linda Davelos."

Linda's step was tentative and she didn't lift her head, so her long hair hid her plump face. A light smattering of applause greeted her.

"Darlene Bryson." The girl in the midnight blue velvet gown decorated with shells stepped forward. She nervously stroked one long, ribbon-wrapped braid. The audience applauded louder and she turned her head to smile her thanks.

"Isabel Redwing."

Tempe wondered if the girl was any relation to Daniel as she stepped beside her fellow contestants with applause following her. The skirt of her silky turquoise gown was decorated with narrow red, white and purple stripes. She wore her light brown hair in a simple, shoulder length cut. Isabel stared straight ahead without smiling.

"And now I'd like to introduce our Princess for the coming year." Two John paused.

Katherine edged closer to the entrance.

"Isabel Redwing!"

Isabel gasped, her eyes opening wide in surprise. The audience clapped wildly as the previous Princess approached Isabel with the crown held out before her. Linda raised her head, a huge smile brightened her round face. She actually looked relieved.

"There must be some mistake!" Katherine gasped. "Linda's supposed to win! How can this be after all I've done?"

"Just what is it that you've done, Mrs. Davelos?" Tempe asked, stepping beside the woman.

"What? Are you speaking to me?"

"Yes, ma'am, I am. What exactly was it that made you so sure your daughter would win this contest?" Tempe grasped Katherine's upper arm.

Katherine's face reflected anger. "I don't know why I should answer that, Deputy."

"Come along with me, Mrs. Davelos. There are some people I'd like you to meet."

Trying to wrest her arm away from Tempe, Katherine said, "I don't want to meet any friends of yours."

Tempe grasped Katherine's arm tighter. "You have no choice, Mrs. Davelos. Come along now."

"What is this? Are you arresting me? What did I do?"

"No, I'm not arresting you as long as you cooperate." Tempe led Katherine from the arena.

"Cooperate? What's going on?"

"You'll find out soon enough," Tempe said.

They approached the picnic tables just as ambulance attendants rolled a gurney through the gate. Katherine stared glumly, keeping her silence.

Hutch and the Celsos weren't anywhere in sight.

Tempe led Katherine to the gate where Deputy

Bradley stood guard. "Go tell one of the detectives I have someone here that they should talk to."

"Detectives!" Katherine exploded. "I'm not talking to anyone without my lawyer."

"If you feel you need a lawyer then you most certainly may have one," Tempe said.

Morrison lumbered toward them from the other side of the fence. "Who's this?"

"Katherine Davelos. She's the mother of one of the other Princess contestants," Tempe explained. "I saw her hurrying away from this direction just before I found the body."

Katherine frowned. "Whose body?"

Ignoring her question, Tempe said, "This is Detective Morrison."

"I'm not talking to anyone until someone lets me in on what the hell is going on." Her mouth opened into a large O. "It's Marella isn't it? My God! Is she dead? Surely you don't think I...." Katherine once again tried to jerk herself free from Tempe's grasp.

Morrison fixed his round, black eyes upon Katherine and she stopped struggling. "You're right, Marella Celso is dead. We aren't accusing you or anyone else yet, Mrs. Davelos, but we would like to ask you a few questions."

"I don't know why you want to spend so much time with me," Katherine said, quickly.

Despite his forbidding appearance, Morrison spoke sweetly, almost cajoling. "We just want to talk to you, ma'am, find out exactly what you do know. Often folks don't give any importance to knowledge that might be very helpful to the case."

His efforts to reassure her didn't have much effect; Katherine shuddered when he said the word "case".

"Why don't you just step inside." Morrison held open the gate for her to enter.

Tempe released Katherine. Without looking back, the woman marched past Morrison. The floodlights had been turned on, illuminating the entire crime scene for those combing the area and beyond for clues.

Just as Katherine and the detective neared the corner of the building, Hutch and the Celsos came around it. Jake Celso supported his wife who leaned heavily upon him as she wept against his shoulder. When Katherine spotted them, she jumped behind Detective Morrison as if using him for a shield.

Totally consumed by their grief, the Celsos took no notice of Katherine, passing by her without so much as a glance in her direction. Katherine peeked around the detective's considerable bulk studying the couple until they passed through the gate.

Tempe quit watching Katherine as Hutch paused for a moment to speak with her. "I'm going to take the Celsos home. Would you arrange for someone to bring their truck?" Hutch gave her a set of keys. "I don't know when I'll get back. I'm going to stay with the Celsos for as long as they need me."

As soon as Hutch and the Celsos disappeared, Grant Whitcomb burst through the nearly deserted entrance, shouting, "One of those filthy, thieving savages stole my gun!"

6

The curious, attracted by the emergency vehicles and personnel, and who remained near the fence instead of going to the grandstands, had been rewarded for their vigilance by the body being brought out, followed by Marella's parents. The crowd now turned their attention to the agitated old man.

Mr. Whitcomb jumped from one foot to the other, his wrinkled face turning a dangerous shade of purple. "It's gone, dagnab it! I tell you it's gone!"

Tempe hurried to his side. "Calm down, Mr. Whitcomb. What kind of a gun was it?"

"You gonna find it for me?" Whitcomb eyed her suspiciously.

"It would help if I knew what to look for," she said.

"A Colt .45. Got a six-inch barrel."

Exactly like the gun that had been beside Marella! "When did you last have your gun?" Tempe asked.

Whitcomb lowered his eyes and shuffled his feet.

"If you want me to help you, Mr. Whitcomb, then you're going to have to give me some information."

He glared at the people who had pressed closer to him and Tempe, obviously eavesdropping. "What's the matter with you, didn't your mothers teach you no manners?"

The small crowd shrank back a few steps but kept their attention on him.

"Dadburn Indians...ain't got no upbringing at all!"

Tempe sighed. "Mr. Whitcomb, it doesn't look to me like many of those folks are Indians."

"They may not look like it, but you can bet they are. Why else would they be here?"

"Why did you come, Mr. Whitcomb?"

"Since my gun got stolen, I been wondering the same thing myself."

"Tell me about your gun. Where was it?"

Again Whitcomb shuffled his feet.

"Well?"

He mumbled so quietly, Tempe had to strain to hear. "I had it in my pocket."

Tempe had been right about the bulge she'd noticed in his overalls earlier. But the last time she'd seen him, it was no longer there. "When did you realize the gun was missing?"

Lowering his head again, he said, "I don't know."

"You weren't aware when someone lifted a big weapon like that from your pocket!" Tempe was incredulous.

"Maybe you ain't noticed, Deputy, but I'm getting old. I ain't as sharp as I used to be," he snarled.

Tempe decided not to comment. He might be sharper than anyone gave him credit. Maybe he killed Marella to hurt Jake. If it was his gun it could be identified easily, saying it was stolen was the smart thing to do. But he'd have to make sure that it could be proven that it had occurred before Marella was killed.

And Tempe could do that.

"Come with me, Mr. Whitcomb. I think I know where your gun is." She took hold of his elbow.

"Yeah? Where's that?"

Tempe didn't say anything as she guided him through the small gathering as they parted to let them pass. Deputy Bradley stared curiously as he opened the gate for them.

"Hey! Wait a minute," Whitcomb said, trying to dig in his heels. "Something bad happened back here. You ain't gonna rope me in on nothing."

"I'm just going to show you where your gun is," Tempe said.

Reluctantly, Whitcomb limped along beside her. Detective Richards became aware of their approach first. "Who's this, Crabtree?"

"Grant Whitcomb, Detective Richards."

The detective squinted at Whitcomb. "What's the story?"

"Mr. Whitcomb lost his Colt .45. I told him I

thought I knew where it was," Tempe said.

Richards kept on squinting at the old rancher. "How'd you lose a big gun like that?"

Whitcomb squirmed. "I had it in my pocket."

"What do you think happened to it? Did it just fall out, and you not notice?" Richards sounded sarcastic.

"No, damn it, it couldn't have fallen out. It was right here." Whitcomb stuck his hand into a deep pocket.

"So what did happen to it, then?"

"One of these no-good Indians stole it."

"You got any idea which one it might be?"

Whitcomb shook his head. "But they don't have no problem stealing my cows and horses, they sure ain't gonna worry about helping themselves to my gun."

"Oh," Richards said, "you're that Whitcomb."

Morrison stepped beside Richards. "What've we got here?"

"Mr. Whitcomb says he lost his gun. A Colt .45."

"Oh yeah?" One hairy eyebrow shot upward. "We just might have your gun, Mr. Whitcomb. Why don't you step over here with me and see if you can identify it?"

Whitcomb looked at Tempe like he was almost frightened to accompany the huge Morrison. But she didn't know if it was because of Morrison's formidable appearance, or because Whitcomb didn't want to see his gun.

When they were out of hearing range, Richards leaned near Tempe. "What's the story on this guy? What business did he have at the Pow Wow? He have any interest in the victim?"

Tempe told him about Whitcomb's prejudice against Indians, his ongoing feud with the Celso family, and being at the Pow Wow for no apparent reason except to agitate Jake and himself. "I can't imagine he'd go so far as to kill Marella just to get back at her father but...."

"I'll be wanting to talk to you about all this in more detail later, Crabtree." Richards turned his back on her and started over to where Morrison and Whitcomb stood near the place where Tempe had found Marella's body.

Tempe knew she'd been dismissed. The detectives never let the lowly deputies in on what was going on. Because Whitcomb hadn't immediately been sent on his way though, she could be pretty sure the gun that had been found next to Marella belonged to the rancher.

Since it must be getting close to the time for the Pow Wow to end, Tempe decided to head back to the arena. She still had to arrange for someone to drive the Celso's truck back to the reservation.

As she once again passed through the folks standing just outside the fence, she was aware of their questioning glances but tried not to make eye contact with any of them.

"Hey, Deputy!" someone hollered from the outside fringe. "What's going on? Is it true someone was murdered?"

Tempe focused on the questioner and recognized him immediately, a reporter from the Dennison newspaper. In his mid-twenties, his hair cut in a short, popular style that made him look even younger, the man made his way to Tempe. An expensive looking camera hung around his neck.

"Daryl Crew." He introduced himself and pointed out his press card clipped to the pocket of his green and yellow striped polo shirt.

"There isn't anything that I can report to you at this time. You'll have to talk to the detectives on the scene." Tempe tried to brush past him, but stepping backwards he kept up with her.

"Aw, come on, Deputy. You know they're just going to tell me to wait for a statement from headquarters. The ambulance attendants already told me they hauled a body out of here. The least you can do is tell me what happened."

Tempe smiled at his perseverance. "You know I can't."

She turned away, intending to march off. From the corner of her eye, she spotted movement from behind the restroom. There was no reason for anyone to be back there.

Without explaining, she darted around the men's side of the building, knowing whoever had been hiding in the shadows would have to come around that way. She didn't want the person to escape through the exit before she had a chance to find out why he or she was hiding.

"Hey, Deputy," Daryl hollered after her. "Where you going?"

Tempe hoped his shout hadn't alerted her target. Just as she reached the corner of the block house, someone dashed toward her with a hand reaching out.

"Hey!" she yelled, side-stepping out of the way. She immediately recognized the Indian outfit and the person wearing it. Daniel Redwing.

He had no intention of slowing down. She grabbed him around the waist while sticking her foot in front of his ankle. He pitched forward. She released him and he fell to his hands and knees. She threw herself on top of him, collapsing him to the ground.

"Put your hands behind your back!" Tempe gasped, as she lifted herself to a kneeling position beside Redwing.

Instead of complying, Redwing rolled away from her and scrambled to his feet.

"Hey!"

Redwing darted toward the exit with Tempe right behind him. The agile Indian plowed into a fat man, knocking him off balance. The man teetered one way and then the other, effectively blocking her. Just as she started around him, the man tumbled over, knocking Tempe to the ground.

She struggled to free her legs from his consider-able bulk.

"What the...." the man gasped.

When Tempe was finally able to follow the fleeing Redwing through the exit turnstile, she couldn't spot him. She scanned the parking lot and the street, but he wasn't anywhere to be seen. No vehicles were driving away.

Frustrated, she whirled around to re-enter the fair-ground and nearly bumped into the reporter right behind her. "Sorry, didn't know you were there. Did you happen to see where he disappeared?"

"Who?" Crew asked.

"The man I was chasing, of course," Tempe snapped.

Crew grinned. "And who might that be? The murderer?"

Exasperated, Tempe said, "Did you see where he went or not?"

Crew shook his head. "'Fraid not, you and that big moose pretty much blocked the way."

There was nothing she could do but go back inside and report to the detectives what had happened, adding Daniel Redwing to their growing list of suspects because of his actions.

As usual, Morrison and Richards accepted the information and dismissed her without displaying any interest or revealing what they planned to do with it. Because a number of people were making their way from the grandstand area, Tempe knew the Pow Wow must be over. She still had to arrange for someone to take the Celsos' truck to their house, and she wanted to ask Nick Two John and Abel Contreras what else they might know about Daniel Redwing.

The exiting crowd flowed around her as she neared the arena. Linda Davelos rushed toward her, her round face troubled. "Deputy, I need to talk to you."

Tempe halted. "What is it?"

"Not out in the open like this. Someone might hear." With a swish of her green satin gown, white fringe swaying, Linda hiked off in her white knee high boots. Curious, Tempe followed.

Linda led her to the empty booth where the craft demonstrations had been given. A line creasing her wide forehead, the girl said, "You've got to tell me the truth."

"What about?"

"Is Marella really dead?"

Though it wasn't up to Tempe to make the announcement, she didn't think it would hurt the investigation to answer the question. "Yes, Linda, I'm afraid she is."

The girl made a slight moaning sound, and shut her eyes briefly. When she opened them, they were misty, her eyelashes moist. "What happened to her?"

Before long the cause of Marella's death would be public knowledge. "She was shot."

Linda took a deep breath before speaking again. "Did my mother kill her?"

7

"I'm afraid I don't know the answer to that," Tempe said. She had a lot of questions she wanted to ask Linda but knew she'd have to be careful how she went about it.

Before she could ask the first one, the shrill voice of Katherine Davelos interrupted. "There you are, Linda! What are you doing over here? What's going on, Deputy?"

"Nothing, Mother," Linda mumbled, hanging her head, her long brown hair hiding her face.

"It's time to go, come along, Linda." She hooked her arm through her her daughter's, and without so much as a glance in Tempe's direction, lifted her chin high and led Linda away.

Tempe considered Linda's question. Did Katherine Davelos kill Marella? She was hurrying away from the direction of the body just before Tempe discovered it. It wouldn't be the first time a mother killed her daughter's competition. Tempe couldn't help but wonder what all the detectives had found out from

Katherine before releasing her.

Realizing she still had to find someone to return the Celsos car, Tempe made her way through the remaining groups of Indians. She found Nick Two John gathering papers into a briefcase. "I'm glad I caught you," she said.

"I won't be going anywhere for awhile," Nick said. "What can I do for you, Crabtree?"

"Hutch took the Celsos home." She fished their keys out of her pocket. "I need to find someone to drive their truck for them."

"That's easy. Hey, Abel."

Contreras was on the bandstand dismantling the sound system. "Yo."

"Would you drive the Celsos' truck home?"

Though he stared at Tempe curiously, he didn't voice his questions when he took the keys from her.

"How're they doing?" Two John asked. She knew he meant the Celsos.

"They're taking it pretty hard. Hutch is with them."

"Good. He'll be able to help them as much as anyone could. You know who did it yet?"

Tempe shook her head. "I'm not investigating the case. It's not my job."

Two John grinned at her. "Never knew that to stop you before."

"There really isn't much I can do, Nick. The detectives aren't going to share any of their information with me and I just can't go nosing around on my own."

"Uh huh." He lifted his straight black eyebrows.

A young male dancer, his regalia decorated with eagle feathers, greeted Two John and stepped behind the tables to retrieve a box. He reminded Tempe of something.

"Have you seen Cody Endrezza? I was supposed to tell him the detectives wanted to speak with him."

Two John frowned. "I haven't seen Cody for a while. I wonder if he even knows about Marella. This is really going to tear him up. He was planning on marrying her."

"That's what Violet told me." Tempe remembered the confrontation between Marella and Cody that she'd witnessed.

"I better go tell the detectives I couldn't find Cody. And if you don't need me for anything, I'll take off as soon as Morrison and Richards say it's okay."

Two John shrugged his broad shoulders. "Place is pretty well cleared out. Thanks for your help. Hope you learned something."

"It was quite an experience, Nick. See you back in Bear Creek."

Morrison was tucking his notebook into his jacket pocket when Tempe approached him. "Sorry, but I couldn't find Cody Endrezza anywhere."

Richards squinted at her. "Who's that?"

"Marella's boyfriend."

"Oh, yeah." He didn't look particularly interested. "Remember I told you about overhearing them having a quarrel earlier this evening. And the outfit he wore was decorated with eagle feathers." Tempe knew the feather that had been near the body had been collected as evidence.

"Are you hinting at something, Crabtree?" Morrison asked.

"Not at all. I just think Endrezza is someone you ought to talk to."

"Thank you." Morrison looked amused. "Was there something else?"

"Not really. If you don't need me for anything, then I guess I'll head back to Bear Creek."

"Why don't you do that." Morrison cupped the elbow of one of his bulky arms while propping his immense jaw with the other hand.

Tempe drove the twenty miles from the Dennison fairgrounds to Bear Creek, her mind busily sorting out the events of the day and evening. Even though she wouldn't be part of the ongoing investigation of Marella's murder, she couldn't help speculating.

The night was clear with a full moon. And as she left the valley floor, it became easier to see the stars studding the sky. The highway curved past orange groves and passed over one end of a small lake. Tempe slowed the Blazer as she passed the campground, noting only a few fires, signifying most of the campers had already turned in.

She increased her speed because she was anxious to get home. Rocky pastures and hillsides garnished with varieties of oaks gave way to more rugged mountains and cedar and pine trees. Before coming to the actual town of Bear Creek, Tempe turned onto a small road, crossed the bridge over the river, and made another turn down a narrow lane.

Pulling into her driveway, she parked behind Hutch's truck and Blair's bright yellow VW Bug. A warm glow came from the kitchen windows of her small cottage. She smiled. Maybe Hutch was waiting up for her.

When she opened the side door into the kitchen, Hutch jumped up from where he'd been sitting at the table and greeted her with a kiss and a breathtaking hug.

"I hoped that was you. Want some coffee?" he asked when he released her.

He poured her a cup and they sat opposite each other, holding hands across the table. "Anything new happen after I left?"

"As a matter of fact, yes. Isabel Redwing was crowned Princess."

"That must have been a surprise to Katherine Davelos," Hutch said.

"She certainly wasn't very happy about it."

"Do you think she had anything to do with Marella's death?"

"It's hard for me to imagine a mother killing her daughter's competition for a title like Pow Wow princess, but there have been similar murders and murder plots." Tempe sipped her coffee. "There are other suspects."

"Really?" Freckles dusted his cheeks and the bridge of his nose.

"Grant Whitcomb claims someone stole his gun out of his pocket."

"What on earth was he doing with a gun at the Pow Wow?"

"Good question. It looks like it was the gun that killed Marella. The detectives probably know for sure by now."

"Do you think he's telling the truth, that someone did steal his gun?"

Tempe shrugged. "I have no idea. But I do know that he hates the Celsos enough to do almost anything to hurt them. Whether that includes killing their daughter, I don't know."

Hutch pulled off his glasses and massaged the bridge of his nose. "I can't imagine what that kind of information will do to Jake. He's having a hard enough time dealing with Marella's death as it is."

"That isn't all. I spotted Daniel Redwing hiding out near the murder scene. When I went after him, he bolted. I couldn't catch up with him."

"Isn't he the one you escorted out of the fairgrounds earlier?"

"Obviously he returned. Maybe to kill Marella. Running off like he did makes me wonder about him."

"Why would he want Marella dead?" Hutch asked.

"I have no idea, but I saw him following Marella around. Maybe he had a crush on her and she wouldn't have anything to do with him."

"How would killing her change that?" Hutch asked. "Want some more coffee?" He stood and went to the stove.

He always made coffee in an old fashioned blue and white pot he'd brought with him from his home. Most of his furnishings and household goods had been sold when he moved to Tempe's, but he said nothing made coffee quite as tasty as his old pot.

"Keeps anyone else from having her." Tempe thought of the television and movie stars who had been stalked and injured or killed by obsessed fans.

"My goodness, that's quite an impressive collection of suspects." Hutch refilled both of their cups.

"There's one more."

Hutch slid back into his chair and once again took Tempe's hand in his. "And who is that?"

"Cody Endrezza. He just kind of disappeared."

"I can help you out with that one. He turned up at the Celsos' soon after we arrived. He's pretty distraught. When I left he and the Celsos were consoling one another. I doubt if he had anything to do with Marella's death."

"Poor people. I know it has to be terrible to deal with the death of a child." The death of her husband had been the worst thing that Tempe had ever experienced. Milt had been her whole life, and if it hadn't been for Blair she couldn't have made it. But her son needed her, and somehow she'd gone on.

Hutch squeezed her hand. It was almost as though he knew what she was thinking about. He smiled at her, deepening the dimple in his cheek. "A death of a loved one is always difficult....and even more so when it's unexpected and violent." Tempe knew he meant that as much for her as a comment about the Celsos.

She smiled at him. It was hard for her to believe that when she'd known Hutch during her growing up years that she'd considered him somewhat of a nerd. Maturity had bestowed him with an attractiveness that was missing in his youth.

"I'm going to help with Marella's funeral," he said.

"Really?" Tempe was surprised as she'd expected them to have some sort of ritualistic Indian ceremony.

"Marella was a Christian which will make my task much easier. I'll be working with one of the elders from the reservation who is also a Christian."

"When is it going to be held? I'd like to go."

"They haven't decided yet, but I think the Celsos would be pleased if you came."

If the bereaved parents were anything like she'd been at Milt's funeral, they probably wouldn't have much memory of who was in attendance until they read the guest book. But Tempe would like to see who turned up. It would also give her a chance to find out some of the answers to the questions that still bothered her.

"There is one thing though...." Hutch began. "I hope you aren't going to take it upon yourself to go snooping around."

Hutch's remark surprised her.

He continued. "I know you can't stand an un-solved mystery but, Tempe, how about leaving this one up to your friends, Morrison and Richards."

"I can't believe you said that. You know how I feel about those two. They'll just take the easiest way out even if it means arresting the wrong person for the murder." Tempe felt her anger rise.

Hutch came around the table and helped Tempe to her feet. "I'm jealous of all the time you spend away from me. We are newlyweds, after all. Do you realize this is the first time since our honeymoon that you've been here so early on a Saturday night? Usually I'm sound asleep by the time you get home."

Grinning, Tempe said, "That's right. So what are we doing sitting out here wasting our time, when we could be making love."

Hutch put his arm around her and nuzzled her cheek. "That's my whole point."

As they walked past Blair's room, Tempe peeked inside. Her son sprawled across the top of his rumpled sheets, long muscular legs akimbo. A slight breeze came in the open window, rustling the curtains and rumpling his corn silk hair. Tempe blew him a kiss as she closed his door.

Hutch put his arm around her waist and hugged

her close to him. "I'm so glad you're my wife." Before she could say anything, he'd covered her mouth with his and kissed her deeply.

When he released her, she smiled at him. "And I'm glad you're my husband. I love you so much." She hadn't realized how lonely her life had been until Hutch had come into it.

Even though she had to work most evenings, when she came in at night, though still asleep, Hutch opened his arms to her, holding her close through the night. Mornings he was always the first one up. By the time she awakened, Hutch had sent Blair off to school, done some of the chores, and had breakfast ready for her. He always sat with her while she ate, drinking more coffee, asking questions about her shift, and telling funny stories about members of his flock.

The two evenings a week she didn't work they spent together, sometimes going out, more often spending the time in quiet conversation, watching something special on TV, playing games by themselves or with Blair.

Sunday morning, Hutch brought coffee to Tempe and perched on the edge of the bed as she sipped it. He reached out and stroked her hair. "I love your hair when it's down."

She nuzzled his bare shoulder. All he wore was a pair of faded cutoffs. "Got time to climb back in bed?" she asked.

He slid his hand down her arm. "Wish I did. I

don't think my congregation would appreciate me being late for church...especially because I was fooling around with my wife."

"But it's so much fun," she teased, knowing he'd never give in.

"Shame on you, tempting a preacher." Hutch grinned and leaned over to kiss her. "Time I took a shower and got into my Sunday-go-to-meeting clothes."

"We could always take a shower together...save time and water," she suggested.

He laughed and pulled away from her. "I doubt we'd save a bit of either one. Are you coming to church today?"

"Wouldn't miss it." Unless she'd had a particularly difficult night, she made it a habit to attend church. Not able to do any of the other minister's wife's duties, she did at least want to make an appearance at the service. Besides, she loved to hear Hutch preach.

"What about Blair, is he up yet?"

"Up and gone. Went on a call. Said he'd meet us at church if he got through in time." Hutch disappeared into the bathroom and the shower came on.

Blair did turn up at the chapel and in celebration of being together, the family went out for dinner at the local cafe. Blair monopolized the conversation, describing the accident he'd worked on. Before they'd finished eating, Blair's pager sounded and he was off again.

After a peaceful afternoon, Tempe went to work. Sunday evenings were usually quiet, even in the summer, and this one was no exception. She didn't even have to make a traffic stop. After calling in her report to the dispatcher in Dennison, she headed home.

Again, her husband and son's vehicles were in the driveway. She parked the Blazer behind them. The cottage was dark. No one waited up for her.

Though it was doubtful anyone would ever tamper with it or its contents while it was parked near her home, because the Blazer belonged to the department, she locked the doors.

As she turned toward the house, a dark shape broke away from the deep shadows of the large fir tree in the front yard.

8

"Deputy, can I talk to you...please?" A masculine voice asked.

She waited for the man to step nearer to see if she recognized him. Long brown hair had been slicked back into a pony tail, a heavy brow overshadowed deep-set eyes. It was Daniel Redwing clad in a faded red sleeveless sweatshirt and well-worn Levi's.

Tempe felt a twinge of anger. "Why did you run from me, Redwing?"

"I dunno, just got scared I guess."

"What do you want?"

"Heard there's a warrant out for my arrest."

"There very well may be." Tempe hadn't received that information yet, but the Dennison sub-station treated Bear Creek and its resident deputy like un-loved step-children. "Are you turning yourself in to me?"

Redwing took a step backwards. "Not exactly."

"What are you here for then?" If there was a warrant, Tempe ought to arrest him right then. But she was tired, and he'd probably just take off again. It made more sense to find out why he'd sought her out.

Swiping at his hair, Redwing cleared his throat. "Do you think maybe we could talk inside?"

"Sure." She guessed he must have a lot to say.

As she led the way into the kitchen, Tempe pointed to a chair. "You want something to drink? A soda, maybe?"

"Uh uh." He dropped into the offered seat.

Tempe sat across the table from him. "Look, Redwing, I've just finished working more hours than usual and I'm worn out. Could you tell me the reason you're here?"

"Is it true they think I killed Marella?" He looked anxious.

"I have no idea who they think killed her. The detectives don't keep me informed about their murder investigation. But they probably want to ask you some questions. The way you took off on me makes you look suspicious."

"I didn't do it. I would never have hurt Marella. I loved her." Redwing's voice quavered and his dark eyes were moist.

"But she didn't love you, did she, Daniel?"

"Not yet. But she would have come around some-day, I know she would."

"Her mother told me Marella planned to marry Cody Endrezza."

Redwing's voice rose, "I don't know why Marella liked Cody."

"Quiet," Tempe cautioned. "My family is asleep."

"Sorry." He leaned over the table toward her. "You gotta believe me, Deputy. I didn't do it!"

"Why'd you run?"

"I watched when they brought her body out. 'Course I didn't know who it was until I saw her folks. I hoped it wasn't her but knew it was. I felt terrible. There wasn't any reason for me to hang around any longer, but when I started to leave, you tackled me. I wasn't thinking straight, all I wanted to do was get out of there." While he spoke, he twisted his fingers.

"You're going to have to tell all that to the detectives, Daniel."

"Yeah, I know."

Hutch, wearing a terry cloth robe and baggy shorts, his thatch of auburn hair tousled from sleep, came from the hall. He blinked his near-sighted eyes. "What's going on in here?"

"Hi, honey," Tempe said. "We've got a visitor. This is Daniel Redwing."

Hutch frowned. "Isn't he the one..."

Tempe finished for him. "Who ran away from me at the Pow Wow but has decided he ought to talk to me after all. Daniel, this is my husband, Hutch Hutchinson. He's the pastor of the Bear Creek Community Church."

"Hi, Daniel." Hutch offered his hand.

Redwing glowered and shrank away from him. "I don't have any use for white men, especially white men who are preachers."

"Sorry," Hutch said. He sat down between Tempe and Redwing. "Mind telling me why?"

"You white men only sees us as Indians...not as people," Redwing snarled.

Hutch put his arm around Tempe. "Not this white man."

"You're still a preacher. Made a promise to myself never to have any more dealings with preachers."

"Preachers are individuals just like Indians," Hutch said.

"That's not the way I see it. You think your ways are right and ours are wrong."

Hutch smiled kindly. "Why don't you tell me exactly what you mean?"

Redwing made a rude snorting noise. "You're just trying to trick me, get me to say something you can use against me."

Hutch held out his hands, palms upwards. "Maybe my wife might use something you say against you, but I promise you I've got no such motives. You don't have to explain anything to me. I merely wondered what experience caused you to be so against ministers."

The young man stared at Hutch for a long time before speaking. "Once I went to one of your kind for help with my drinking problem. He condemned our way of burning offerings of sweet grass and sage. Said it was an abomination to the Lord. Told me the smell was nothing but a stench to God."

Hutch shook his head, making no comment.

"I don't believe in your God anyway. I only believe in the Great Spirit, our Creator."

"I'm sure that He is the same person," Hutch said. "God has many names. No matter what we choose to call Him, He loves us all the same."

Redwing stared at Hutch but didn't speak.

"What do you want me to do for you, Daniel?" Tempe asked.

He shoved his chair back and stood. "I just wanted you to know I didn't kill Marella."

"Okay." Tempe rose slowly. "I suppose I really ought to arrest you and take you in tonight."

Redwing glanced over his shoulder toward the door.

Tempe continued. "But I won't as long as you'll promise to turn yourself in first thing tomorrow. It won't help you any to keep running, it just makes you look guilty."

"Right. That's what I'll do." He backed up until his hand was on the door.

"My wife is giving you good advice, son," Hutch said.

Redwing said nothing more. He yanked open the door and disappeared into the night.

"Troubled young man," Hutch said. "Do you think

he did it?"

Tempe shrugged. "I don't know, and frankly, I'm too tired to even worry about it now. All I want to do is fall into bed."

"Come along then." As he escorted her toward their bedroom, he said, "You know, I'd like to spend some time with that young man. Perhaps I could help him."

Tempe grinned. "Because you'd like to change his opinion of preachers."

"That too."

It seemed as though Tempe had just fallen asleep when the phone woke her. Because it only rang a couple of times, she knew Hutch had answered it, and she turned over on her stomach and burrowed into her pillow.

"Tempe, I'm sorry to have to wake you," Hutch said. "But Sergeant Guthrie's on the phone. He says it's important."

Without opening her eyes, Tempe reached out for the receiver. "Crabtree here," she mumbled.

"We're having a meeting this morning about the Celso murder. Richards and Morrison have requested that you attend." No greeting, no apology for disturbing her on her day off--typical Sergeant Guthrie.

"What time?" She sighed, and swung her legs over the side of the bed.

Hutch stood just inside the door. "Do you want your coffee now?"

Tempe nodded, and her husband hurried off.

"Can you make it by nine?" the Sergeant asked.

The bedside clock radio read five after eight. "I'll try."

The Sergeant hung up.

Tempe pulled a fresh uniform from the closet and tossed it on the bed. Pulling her nightgown over her head, she hurried to the bathroom. She was in the shower when she heard Hutch.

"Obviously, you have to go to work. Will you have time for breakfast?"

"No. Sorry."

"I put your coffee on the counter."

"Thanks, Sweetheart. I love you."

"I love you too."

She heard him go out. After dressing quickly, she towel-dried and brushed out her long, black hair. Though it was still damp, she quickly braided it into a long queue which she folded and fastened to the back of her head with a large barrette.

Peering at her face, as usual she decided against putting on any make-up. Not just because she didn't have much time, but also because her black brows and lashes didn't need darkening, and her high cheekbones still had a pinkish glow from sleep. She quickly covered her full lips with gloss and hurried toward the kitchen.

"You look beautiful as always," Hutch said after greeting her with a kiss. "Wish you had time for a real breakfast. But I did fix you a bite to take with you." He held out a bagel on a napkin, the cut halves generously spread with cream cheese.

Tempe laughed. "You're such a sweetie. "Maybe this won't take too long and we'll still have time to do something together when I get back."

Smiling apologetically, Hutch said, "I promised the Celsos I'd come out to the reservation today and meet with the tribal council. Seems I'll need their okay to help officiate at the funeral. And I also wanted to stop by the Celsos and see how they're doing."

"Of course. We'll still have our evening together." Tempe kissed him goodbye and headed out to the Blazer. When she saw the VW was gone, she realized she hadn't even asked about Blair. Not only had she turned over the majority of her homemaking chores to Hutch, she seemed to be letting him do more and more of the parenting. When she glanced at her watch she knew she didn't have time to feel guilty.

It was nine o'clock exactly when she pulled into the parking lot of the rectangular building that housed the sheriff's substation in Dennison. She hurried up the stairs to the porch that led to the side door that was only used by the deputies and other employees.

The heels of her boots clicked on the worn and dirty linoleum, and the creaking of her leather utility belt echoed in the long narrow hallway. Tempe made her way past the many doors to the one that opened into Sergeant Guthrie's office.

It was little more than a cubicle even though the Sergeant was the ranking officer. As usual, his scarred and battered desk was piled high with books and papers. The one bookcase overflowed with notebooks and folders. The dirty, drab walls were decorated with wanted posters, typed announcements, law enforcement posters, and jokes.

Detectives Morrison and Richards were already seated in the two padded chairs, leaving the metal folding chair for her. They both cast her an irritated glance and a slight nod for a greeting. Though it was only two minutes past the hour, they acted as though she'd kept them waiting for a long time.

"Let's get right to work," Guthrie said, barely glancing at her as he smacked his meaty palms on the open folder in front of him. "Morrison tells me you found the murder victim."

"Yes, sir." She briefly explained the circumstances. Guthrie listened carefully, his bushy graying brows nearly meeting over his small, but intelligent eyes.

"Nobody was around?" Guthrie asked.

"Not at the scene. But like I told the detectives, just before discovering the body, I did see Katherine Davelos coming from that direction," Tempe said, questions of her own filling her brain.

"Who's that?" the Sergeant asked.

Morrison sighed loudly; Richards shoved his chair against the wall and stretched out his long legs.

"The murder victim was the candidate for Pow

Wow Princess most likely to win. Mrs. Davelos was really pushing her own daughter."

"Did she want her kid to win bad enough to kill the competition?" Guthrie asked.

"I wouldn't put it past her," Tempe said.

"Did you question this Davelos woman?" The Sergeant looked from one detective to the other.

"Of course," Richards said. "She may have had a motive, but I don't think she did it."

"Maybe she hired someone to kill Marella," Tempe suggested.

Richards ignored her. "At this time, our primary suspect is Daniel Redwing. He lives on the reservation, but we haven't been able to locate him as yet."

"There's something I have to tell you," Tempe put in quickly.

Richards squinted at her and Morrison put his hands behind his round head and yawned.

"Go ahead," the Sergeant said. At least he didn't look bored.

"Daniel Redwing came to my house early this morning."

Richards sat up straight and Morrison's mouth gaped.

"And you didn't arrest him?" Richards said.

"What for? No one told me he was wanted for anything."

"You're the one he got away from, doesn't it seem reasonable that if he ran from you he must have had something to hide?" Morrison growled.

"But that doesn't prove that he killed Marella." Tempe crossed her arms and stared at them.

"For crap's sake, Crabtree. You had the suspect in your grasp and you didn't have sense enough to bring him in?" Anger made Morrison even uglier than usual.

"Hey!" Guthrie snapped. "Why don't you give Crabtree a chance to tell us what happened?"

Tempe smiled at the Sergeant before launching into a detailed report of Redwing's visit. The only thing she left out was the interchange between him and Hutch.

Richards leaned forward. "The way I see it, this Redwing was obsessed with Marella Celso. Tempe told us herself that he'd been following the girl around at the Pow Wow. But she was in love with someone else. Sometime during the day, he lifted old man Whitcomb's gun. After he'd been thrown out for drinking, Redwing sneaked back in and laid in wait for the Celso girl and killed her."

"That's what I think too." Morrison flashed a self-satisfied grin in Tempe's direction. "And when we get our hands on this guy, that's what he's gonna tell us."

"Did you get any fingerprints off the gun?" Sergeant Guthrie asked.

"Nothing, of course," Richards said.

"What about Grant Whitcomb?" Tempe asked.

"There's always been bad blood between him and the Celsos. And after all, the gun does belong to him. Why didn't he report it stolen as soon as he discovered it was missing...if that's what really happened."

Morrison's expression revealed that he felt it a waste of time to respond. "We questioned the old man. He says he didn't do it."

"That's what Daniel Redwing says too," Tempe said.

"Why are you defending him, Crabtree?" Richards asked. "Because you made a mistake by not arresting him? Or is it because he's an Indian?"

Tempe shook her head and rolled her eyes. "He said he would come in this morning. If he does, will that change your mind about him?"

Morrison snorted. "He ain't gonna show up anywhere around here. We're gonna have to go to the reservation and dig him out of there, and you know it."

The phone on Guthrie's desk rang, interrupting the debate. Guthrie answered it, listened, and grinned. After replacing the receiver, he said, "Looks like Tempe was right about this one, guys. Redwing just turned himself in."

9

In their rush to get out of the room, the detectives nearly knocked Tempe out of her chair. Sergeant Guthrie stared at her as though he wondered why she was still there.

"If you don't mind, Sergeant, I have some questions."

Guthrie brushed the top of his gray crew-cut and leaned back. "Is it going to be necessary to remind you that it isn't your job to investigate the murder?"

She shook her head. "I'm just curious about something. When they examined Marella, did they find any money?"

The bushy eyebrows shot upward. "Money?"

"She'd been carrying around a good-sized roll of bills. Mostly ones, I'd guess. From the raffle tickets she'd been selling. That's how the Princess was chosen...whoever sold the most tickets."

Guthrie shuffled through the papers in the folder on his desk. He picked one up. After scanning it, he said, "All that was found was a partial book of tickets in one of the pockets of her dress."

"No stubs?"

Frowning, the Sergeant shook his head.

"There should have been stubs and money, unless she turned everything in before she got killed. That's possible, I suppose." Tempe thought for a moment. "But if that were the case, the ticket book would have been new without any tickets gone from it."

As he scribbled on a notebook page, he said, "I'll check it out, Crabtree. Anything else?"

"I know it isn't any of my business, but what else did they get from the murder scene?"

Guthrie folded his hands on top of the papers. "Okay, Crabtree. Here's what we know so far. Because there was no sign of a struggle, we're assuming the victim knew her murderer and didn't feel threatened. From the angle of the shot, we know that the killer was taller than the victim. That's about it."

"When do you expect the autopsy report?" Tempe asked, knowing she was pushing it.

"Maybe later today but probably not until tomorrow." Irritation had crept into Guthrie's voice. He stood, towering over her, one of the few men who could make her feel small. "Anything else?"

She stood too. "Could you let me know if there's anything interesting in it?"

"We don't expect any surprises. This is your day off, Crabtree, don't you have anything to do?"

"Just one more thing, Sergeant. My husband is helping with Marella's funeral...and I'll be going with him."

He leaned over his desk toward her and shook a sausage like index finger at her. "Leave the investigating up to the detectives, Crabtree. I didn't think you'd be tempted since this one is out of your territory."

"Yes, sir." Tempe grinned at him before hurrying from the room.

She didn't plan to go out of her way to investigate, but it wouldn't hurt anything to keep her eyes and ears open while she was at the funeral. Morrison and Richards were always in such a big hurry to close a case, they didn't take the time Tempe thought they should to consider each suspect. And it certainly didn't look like they planned to operate any differently this time. Though she didn't have the slightest idea who killed Marella, she didn't think the detectives had enough evidence against Daniel Redwing to convict him. And he certainly wouldn't confess to a crime he didn't commit.

She turned everything she knew about Marella's murder over and over in her mind while she drove home. Neither of her men were there. After she decided to run up to the grocery store in town and buy some salad greens and steaks for dinner. From the store, she headed toward the outskirts of town to the fire station, hoping to have a chat with Pete Roundtree.

As captain of the Bear Creek Fire Department, Pete knew more about what was going on around town than anyone.

Though she had the day off, her job as resident deputy of Bear Creek meant she was never completely off duty.

Tempe spotted Blair's bright yellow VW Bug parked on the street near the brick building that housed the fire department. A tiny addition had been added onto it that served as Bear Creek's sheriff's office. Tempe seldom used it.

She pulled the Bronco behind her son's Volkswagen and smiled. One of the red fire engines was parked in the driveway. Water and soapsuds flowed over the asphalt. The top of Blair's blond head bobbed up periodically on the other side of the truck as he vigorously scrubbed away the dirt.

Tempe watched him several minutes before he noticed her. At six-foot-three, Blair didn't have any trouble reaching the topmost edges of the vehicle. Husky and strong-jawed, her offspring didn't resemble Tempe at all, except for the blue of his almond shaped eyes. The older he got, the more he looked like his father.

"Wish I could get you to work this hard at home," Tempe said. She laughed and added, "And I wish you spent as much time at home as you do here."

"Hi, Mom." Blair grinned at her but kept on working. "School starts next week, that'll drastically cut down on the time I can hang out here."

"You'll figure out a way." Tempe said. "Pete around?"

Motioning with his head, Blair said, "He's doing paperwork inside."

Pete, Yanduchi like Tempe, was seated behind his desk. When she spoke to him, he grinned, sticking his pen behind one of his big ears. "What's new?"

"That's what I stopped by to ask you."

"Take a seat."

She shook her head. "Have groceries in the car. And that reminds me, send that boy of mine home around six for dinner, will you?"

"He's a great kid, Tempe. Don't know what I'm going to do without him when he's back in school."

"Anything going on up here I ought to know about?" Tempe asked.

"Can't think of a thing."

"Hear about Marella Celso's murder?"

He nodded. "Sad. Celsos are good people. Know who did it yet?"

"Detectives think it was Daniel Redwing. Know him?"

"Sure. Hot-headed kid. Long-haired, got an alcohol problem. Can't figure him killing Marella though. I could believe him brawling with someone...but not shooting a girl like Marella. What would be his reason?"

"Unrequited love." Tempe said. "And that part is

fact. He was crazy about Marella."

"How does killing a girl who doesn't care for you the way you care for her help anything? Doesn't make much sense to me."

"Me neither. But it happens ... and that's how the homicide detectives are figuring it."

"You got someone better in mind?" Pete asked.

"Not yet. But there are others with motives."

"You going to do some detecting on your own?"

"Not supposed to," Tempe said.

"When did that ever stop you?" Pete chuckled.

He had more faith in her than she had in herself. Though she certainly didn't think the investigation should stop at Daniel Redwing, she didn't see how she could do anything since everyone involved in the case lived on the reservation.

"All I'm going to worry about right now is getting home, fixing a big salad and some garlic bread, and putting the steaks I just bought onto the barbecue."

"Tempe Crabtree, housewife."

"You've got that right. It's my day off."

On her way past Blair, who was wiping down the shiny surface of the engine with a chamois, Tempe said, "Try to make it home for dinner. We're having steak." All at once it struck her how fortunate she was to have her only child around to banter with. The Celsos would never again be able to do that with Marella. Somehow she had to do her part to find out who had taken their daughter away from them.

Tempe couldn't keep her mind off Marella Celso's murder but she didn't bring up the subject at the dinner table. It wasn't until after they'd eaten and Blair had dashed off to a brush fire, while she and Hutch were finishing the dishes, that Hutch gave her the opportunity when he said, "They released Marella's body this afternoon. The funeral will be tomorrow."

"That means the preliminary autopsy report is in," Tempe said, not adding that also meant Sergeant Guthrie wasn't planning to let her know what was in it."

"Do you still want to go to the funeral with me?" Hutch put the dishes he'd just dried into the cupboard.

"Of course."

"What are you so preoccupied with?" Hutch frowned at her.

"What? Oh, nothing." She realized she'd been standing with her hands in the nearly cold dishwater, staring out the window without seeing anything. She released the drain stopper, and dried her hands on the towel her husband had been using.

Hutch took her by the shoulders and turned her to face him. "Don't try to fool me, my darling. I've been around you long enough to recognize that look. You're hatching up something."

"I'm just glad I'll have the opportunity to see everyone from the Pow Wow again." She offered her lips to him, hoping to take his mind away from the direction of his query.

He kissed her quickly. "You aren't getting away that easily. You're glad for the opportunity to see everyone connected with Marella's murder. That's what you really mean, isn't it? I heard they arrested Redwing. But you don't think he's guilty, right?"

"I'm not sure. But how can they be so positive when they've barely questioned the others?"

"And you've decided to take it upon yourself to correct the error of their ways."

"Not exactly," Tempe said.

Hutch stared at her, his gray eyes unfaltering.

"Sergeant Guthrie told me not to nose around."

Still not commenting, Hutch continued to stare. The corners of his mouth twitched slightly, his dimple deepening.

"If I'm at the funeral anyway, what could it hurt if I talked to a few people?"

Her husband's face gave way to the smile he'd been suppressing and he pulled her to him, giving her a bear hug. "Won't hurt a thing. I just don't like it when you take time away from us. I sure do love you!"

With his lips brushing her ear, he whispered, "When do you suppose Blair will be back?"

"Do you think there's time?" The mere thought of making love with Hutch caused Tempe's breath to quicken.

Hutch's gray eyes sparkled. "Did you ever know Blair to be in a hurry to get home from a fire?" He ran his fingers down the line of her jaw.

She tingled at his touch. "You're right. We have plenty of time."

Tempe and Hutch had enjoyed a leisurely lovemaking session before settling themselves cozily on the couch in front of the TV. It was a long while before Blair joined them.

Despite her Yanduchi blood, Tempe knew little about the reservation except the way there. She didn't wear her uniform because of the funeral, but they went in the Bronco. Despite the promise of a sultry day ahead, Hutch wore his navy suit. She'd had a hard time finding anything suitable for the occasion, finally settling on a simple, straight line black silk dress with a white lace collar and her low-heeled black pumps. She let her single braid hang down her back instead of her usual manner of fastening it up with a barrette.

Knowing Hutch was mentally preparing himself for the somber occasion, Tempe kept her thoughts to herself as she maneuvered the vehicle up and down and around the many curves of the narrow road. When they first turned off the highway, they passed many small ranches. The houses ranged from Spanish style with arches, porches wrapped around two storied clapboards, large mobile homes, to log cabins.

After a few miles, the terrain became more and more hilly, the ranches larger with the houses farther apart. The closer hills had bare, golden patches. The road followed and crossed the southern branch of Bear Creek several times as it wound its way through the high valley. Oaks, poplars and cottonwood grew along the shallow stream. At times, the grandeur of the Sierra could be glimpsed.

Tempe slowed to allow a small herd of cattle followed by an Indian cowboy on horseback to go around her. A carved wooden sign had been set into a river rock wall. BEAR CREEK INDIAN RESERVATION. Other writing told the reader that Ulysses S. Grant had set aside the land in 1873.

Hutch broke the silence. "This is a beautiful spot isn't it?" Reservation land meandered along both sides of the river, surrounded by sheltering hills which kept the high valley cooler in the summer and protected from the harsher winter storms.

"Isn't it sad to realize this was Marella's home and she'll never see it again?" Tempe sighed and had to blink away a sudden rush of tears.

Hutch reached over and squeezed her hand on the steering wheel.

Houses were scattered over the hillsides, some little more than plywood shacks, yards littered with broken down cars and trucks, others modest, freshly painted bungalows with neat gardens and outbuildings. Within a mile of the entrance, they drove by a large sandstone building with wrought iron grillwork over the windows which Tempe knew belonged to Indian Affairs. Across the way a brick and redwood structure housed the Education Center.

Tempe turned into the lane leading past an empty

playground, heading toward a big white bungalow. A simple cross topped the steep roof. A sign in the yard identified it as the Bear Creek Mission. Several cars already lined the narrow street. A silver hearse was parked at the side. "This must be the place."

With his Bible tucked under one arm, Hutch put his other hand on Tempe's elbow and escorted her inside the vestibule. Double doors opened into the sanctuary. An aisle ran down the center between simple, white painted pews. A few mourners had already taken their places.

"I think I'll sit back here." Tempe said, and slipped into the last row. Easier to see everyone as they entered.

Hutch kissed her lightly. He hurried down the aisle, skirting the gleaming oak coffin which had already been placed in front of a low platform, disappearing through a door off to the side. Floral sprays flanked the open casket, a multitude of flower arrangements and potted plants had been placed along the edge of the platform. Even at the back Tempe was able to smell their cloying sweetness.

A plump woman, probably in her thirties, wearing a dark print dress and glasses, placed several music books on the rack of a spinet piano located on the opposite side of the room from the door Hutch had gone through. She settled herself on the bench, opened one of the books, dramatically arched her wrists over the keyboard and began playing. Someone sniffled.

Several more people entered the church, followed by an even larger group. Within a few minutes the pews were filled. Tempe recognized most of the mourners by sight, though she didn't know many names. At least half of them were young people. Darlene Bryson and Isabel Redwing huddled together, their pretty faces marred by sadness. Linda Davelos preceded her mother into the church. Tempe was surprised Katherine came, as were some of the other mourners judging by the raised eyebrows and startled expressions.

The people in the row in front of Tempe had to squeeze together to make room for the mother and daughter.

A heavy-set man with short black hair, his deep copper face furrowed with wrinkles, appeared in the doorway, at the front. Hutch was right behind him. The piano player began another hymn and two dark-suited men escorted Violet and Jake Celso down the aisle to the first row of the church. The much taller Cody Endrezza, also wearing a suit, followed behind them, his posture almost military, his collar-length hair neatly combed. Before Violet sat down, she stepped over to the casket.

After staring at her daughter for several minutes, Violet leaned over and kissed her. She turned around, her eyes straight ahead, her lips firmly together, not revealing the heartache she must be feeling as she allowed her husband to guide her to their seat. Jake sat on one side of her, Cody on the other.

The two preachers stood in front of the coffin and bowed their heads. The Indian prayed in his native tongue.

Hutch followed with another simple prayer. While he spoke, Tempe felt the presence of someone beside her.

Without raising her head, she opened her eyes. She saw faded Levis, and the scuffed toes of leather boots.

"Do you mind if I sit here?" It was Daniel Red-wing.

10

The funeral had been short; neither the mission pastor nor Hutch had much to say. Hutch focused on the fact that God was in control even though we often are unable to understand His plan, assuring Marella's family and loved ones that she was in a far better place. It was difficult to hear the exact words because of the loud sobbing in the sanctuary.

After everyone filed past the body, the mourners gathered in clumps on the dry grass around the outside of the church. Redwing stood beside Tempe.

"Bet you were surprised to see me," he said. He no longer looked ferocious as he had at the Pow Wow, nor did he seem frightened and troubled as he had when he'd made his surprise visit to her home.

"As a matter of fact, yes."

"They let me go. Didn't have enough evidence to keep me, the public defender said. The detectives told me not to go anywhere." Redwing had slicked his hair back, a leather thong catching it at his neck. He wore a brown sport jacket over an open necked white shirt, the sleeves had been pushed up past his wrists. "Where would I go? Besides, I didn't kill Marella."

"Danny! You made it!" Isabel threw her arms around her brother's neck and began sobbing. "Isn't it awful? I still can't believe Marella's dead."

Daniel pulled away from his sister. She noticed Tempe for the first time and frowned. It took a moment for the girl to realize who she was, no doubt because of her civilian clothes. "Deputy Crabtree? Why are you here? Not because of my brother, I hope."

"Pastor Hutchinson is my husband. I came with him,"Tempe said. "And I wanted to see the Celsos again. Let them know how sorry I am."

Tears brimmed in Isabel's eyes. "Marella was my very best friend. I don't know how I'll get along without her."

If the girls had been best friends, Isabel might know something that could shed some light on the case. "I'd like to talk to you about Marella sometime if you don't mind."

Isabel glanced at her brother. "I don't think..."

"I'd like to know more about her. You might be aware of something important no one else knew. Something that might help us find out who killed her." It was obvious Isabel didn't want to reveal anything that might hurt her brother.

"The deputy knows I didn't shoot Marella," Daniel said.

That wasn't quite true but if his assurance helped give Isabel confidence in Tempe she'd leave it at that.

"Maybe, if you're sure. I'll think about it but I've got to go now. I promised I'd help out at the Celsos. The ladies from the Mission are serving lunch...will you be there?"

"Possibly," Tempe said, not knowing what Hutch's plans were.

She doubted if the Davelos would be welcome at the Celsos'; if she was going to speak with Katherine she'd better do it before she got away. Linda was talking with other girls her age, but it took a few minutes before Tempe spotted her mother.

"Excuse me, there's someone I need to see."

As Tempe moved away from the brother and sister, she heard Isabel say, "Can you believe that Cody? How he wormed his way in with Marella's parents?"

With her hips swinging and her head held high, Katherine made her way around the groups of people. No one seemed to notice her passage. A tight, black leather mini skirt exposed her long, shapely legs. High-heeled ankle-strapped sandals made her nearly as tall as Tempe.

Tempe caught up with Katherine right when she reached her car, an older model Mustang, yellow with black flames painted on the hood. "Mrs. Davelos. May I speak with you for a moment?"

Whirling around to face Tempe, Katherine's mouth dropped open. She blinked her long, artificial lashes.

"Who? Why it's you...the deputy. My, don't you look different." Tempe couldn't tell if her comment was a compliment or criticism--but she didn't care. "Frankly, I was kind of surprised to see you here."

"Why wouldn't I be? Marella was a friend of my daughter's, after all."

"I know you don't get along all that well with Violet Celso."

Katherine sniffed distastefully. "Who'd you hear that from, Violet? She thinks she's so hot. Passes herself off as some sort of expert on Indian lore."

"Seems that's what most of the folks around here think too," Tempe said.

"She's nothing more than an overweight squaw. I probably know as much if not more than she does."

Tempe doubted that. Like Violet had pointed out at the Pow Wow, Katherine's knowledge came from books. Tempe suspected Violet's expertise had been learned from the elders of the reservation. Because of Katherine's attitude and lack of Indian ancestry, Tempe doubted anyone would share information with her.

"Whatever she may be, she's certainly suffered a tragic loss," Tempe said.

Katherine didn't display any sympathy. "Perhaps this will knock her down a peg or two."

Nasty woman, no wonder she didn't seem to have any friends. "The night of the Pow Wow, I saw you coming from the area where I found Marella's body. Do you want to tell me what you were doing over there?"

Narrowing her eyes to slits, Katherine said, "I already told the detectives the answer to that question. I don't have to talk to you." She stomped around to the driver's side of the Mustang. Shading her eyes, she hollered, "Linda! Linda Davelos! Get your butt over here this instant!"

Linda, her head down so that her long hair hid her face, hurried to the car. Tempe stepped back to give her room. Before Linda climbed into the car, she raised her plump face toward Tempe and mouthed the word, "Sorry."

Tempe knew the girl was apologizing for her mother.

The other mourners had begun returning to their vehicles. Hutch stood by the Blazer and waved at her. When she joined him, he said, "We're going to the Celso's for lunch if that's okay with you."

"Sure. But what about the burial?" Tempe asked.

"The internment is going to be later on this afternoon at the cemetery in Dennison. Violet and Jake don't want anyone there with them."

Tempe followed the long line of cars to the Celso's home on one of the side roads. A screened-in porch circled the large green house perched on a flat hillock. At Abel Contreras' direction, Tempe parked the Bronco on the lawn at the side of the house. On top of the steep hillside in back stood a large water tower. A pipe ran down toward the chicken coops, animal pens, and the large vegetable garden in the flat area immediately behind the house. Clothes flapped on a line extending from near the back door.

"Quite a crowd," Tempe said, waiting for Hutch to come around the front end of the vehicle. "How long do you want to stay?"

Hutch took her hand. "As long as it seems like the Celsos need me."

When they entered the screened-in porch, Jake spied them first. He rushed to Hutch with his hands outstretched. "Thanks for coming, Pastor. Can't tell you how much I appreciate you being here." Tears glistened in his eyes. He draped his arm over Hutch's shoulder and led him through open French doors to the darker interior of the house.

Tempe glanced around, seeking a familiar face. She spotted Darlene Bryson standing alone in a plant-filled corner. After making her way through small groups of subdued people, Tempe approached the girl. "Hi, remember me?"

Darlene's long hair curled softly around her face and shoulders. She frowned, showing no recognition.

"I was at the Pow Wow. Deputy Crabtree." Tempe shrugged. "I know I look different without my uniform."

The frown deepened. "Oh, sure, I remember you." But there was a question in her eyes as to what Tempe wanted with her.

"It's terrible what happened to Marella. And I

wondered if there might be anything you'd like to tell me about her."

"I still can't believe it. Everything about her was always so perfect."

"Like what?" Tempe prompted.

"She was so pretty. Everyone liked her. She had super parents and the perfect boyfriend."

"You mean Cody Endrezza?"

Darlene's eyebrows arched. "Of course, Cody."

"What's he like?" '

"You know who he is don't you? He's around here somewhere. He's great looking, and a real nice guy. Marella and he were the perfect couple."

Violet Celso weaved her way between her many friends, acknowledging sympathetic words and touches as she came toward Tempe. Her smile was bright and her eyes clear. "Officer Crabtree, glad you could make it too. I'm afraid Jake isn't doing so well. He's forgotten his manners. Your husband has been most helpful to him...so reassuring. Come along with me, I'll show you where the food is."

Tempe thanked Darlene for talking with her before allowing the shorter woman to guide her inside the house. When her eyes adjusted to the dimmer light, she saw even more folks milling around the long, narrow living room, talking to one another in subdued voices.

"I haven't had the opportunity to tell you how sorry I am about your loss," Tempe said, as they entered the dining room. A great variety of food covered the top of the table.

Violet nodded as she handed Tempe a paper plate. "I hope everyone eats. My friends outdid themselves. There's enough here to feed an army. Be sure and try some of that rice salad. I've had it before and it's delicious." Tempe was surprised by how well Violet seemed to be doing; her thoughts must have shown in her face.

"You have to find something good about any situation you find yourself in. You can't dwell on the negatives. Everyone is sharing our grief...helps make the burden lighter. We have to look forward. Turn what's been done into a better path. Jake will remember that soon, then he will begin to heal as I am healing." Violet hugged her. "Enjoy the food. I'll rescue your husband so he can eat with you." The woman hurried away.

In minutes, Hutch joined her at the bountiful table. "Mrs. Celso is a remarkable woman. No wonder everyone turns to her for guidance. She told Jake he needed to spend time with his friends...and sent me to be with you."

"She has a remarkable attitude considering the circumstances. Some of it is based on her Indian beliefs...but I think a lot has to do with her personal inner strength."

Tempe and Hutch sat down at a tiny table in one corner of the porch to eat their meal. Cody Endrezza meandered through the crowd, his eyes red and swollen as though he'd been crying. He accepted hugs and consoling pats from young and old alike.

Isabel and Daniel Redwing stood near the doorway. Cody glanced at them, but looked away quickly. He side-stepped around them, not acknowledging their presence. Daniel glared at the taller young man as he passed. Isabel put her arm around her brother and pulled him aside. She whispered to him. Daniel yanked himself away, stomping off in the opposite direction.

Isabel briefly glanced after Cody, something in her eyes Tempe couldn't read, before hurrying after her brother.

Tempe patted Hutch's arm. "Excuse me a minute. I think I should try to talk to Isabel before she disappears."

Hutch had been concentrating on his food and hadn't noticed the by-play between the Redwings and Endrezza. His expression changed from puzzled to knowing. "Ah! The sleuth goes to work."

Tempe leaned over and kissed him on the cheek. She caught up with the Redwings outside the house. "Isabel, could I talk to you for a moment?"

"Go on ahead, Danny." She touched her brother's arm. "I'll find someone to bring me home. I promised to stay around and help clean up after everyone leaves." Isabel waved her brother off.

Daniel fixed his black eyes on them for a moment before spinning on his heel and hurrying toward a battered, multi-colored Chevy pick-up.

Isabel glanced around and pointed to a lawn swing beneath an enormous Aspen. "Why don't we sit over there?"

Though the air was still and the temperature had climbed into the high nineties, it felt ten degrees cooler beneath the thick foliage.

"This is nice." Tempe suspected the girl had chosen the spot because of its seclusion rather than the comfort it afforded.

"What do you want to know?"

"How does it feel to be Pow Wow Princess?"

Isabel stared at her hands, twisting her fingers. "I haven't even thought about it. It doesn't seem right. Everyone knew Marella was going to win. I entered because she wanted us to do it together." A tear ran down her cheek. She quickly brushed it away.

"I didn't have the opportunity to get to know Marella. What was she like?"

The girl reached up and pushed her light brown hair behind her ear and sighed. "She is...was nice to everybody. It's no wonder my brother fell for her. A lot of the guys at school have...had crushes on her too."

"Tell me about her relationship with Cody."

"I don't know if I should talk about that. Because we were best friends we told each other things we wouldn't share with anyone else." Isabel turned her head so Tempe couldn't see her face.

"You want us to find out who killed Marella, don't you?"

"I'm just glad they don't think my brother did it anymore."

"That's not necessarily the case, I'm afraid."

Isabel stared at Tempe, her eyes wide. "Surely they wouldn't let him go if they thought he did it, would they?"

"They might not have enough evidence to charge him...yet."

Isabel swallowed a cry. "Oh, my God!"

"Do you want to tell me about Cody and Marella? Everyone says they were going to get married."

Isabel shook her head. "Something happened between them, something that changed Marella's mind. She wasn't going to see Cody anymore."

"No one else seems to know about that." Tempe knew there had definitely been a problem between the two at the Pow Wow.

"Marella hadn't gotten around to telling her folks yet. They like Cody a lot. She was afraid they wouldn't understand."

"What happened, Isabel?"

"I can't tell you." Isabel stood, putting the swing into motion.

"Don't go yet, please. What about your brother and Marella?"

"Danny was crazy about her. When she came to our house, he wouldn't leave her alone. Always staring at her. She said it made her nervous, but I don't really think it bothered her all that much. She was always nice to him."

"Did he ever ask her out?"

"Oh, sure. But she'd just tell him if she wasn't going with Cody, he'd be her next choice."

"Do you think that was true?"

She focused on her hands again. "Not really. And maybe Marella wasn't being fair to Danny. He always thought he had a chance with her."

"Would you say your brother was obsessed with Marella?"

"I don't want to talk about it anymore, Deputy." Isabel started backing away from Tempe. "I loved Marella. So did Danny. He didn't kill her...I know he didn't!" She turned and ran into the house.

Tempe started to follow her, wondering if Hutch was ready to leave yet. Despite all the questions she'd asked, she hadn't learned who killed Marella, not even anything that would make her suspect one more than another.

As she headed toward the house she was surprised to see Daniel's truck was still parked near the end of the lane. But Daniel wasn't in it. He must have changed his mind about leaving. Tempe walked around the porch looking for her husband. She entered the house from the back, excusing her way through the crowded kitchen.

The dishes on the dining room table had been

sampled but there was still an abundance of food.

A loud shout came from the living room, followed by a long, shrill scream. Something crashed. It sounded like a fight had broken out.

"Hey! Stop that you two!" Tempe entered the room just in time to see Daniel pull back his arm, his fist aimed at Cody Endrezza's handsome face.

11

Before Daniel's fist made contact, Hutch grabbed his arm. The taller Cody plunged toward his would-be assailant but Jake came from behind and seized him around the middle, yanking him backwards. Losing his balance, Cody toppled, falling on top of Jake.

Those who had been in the living room scurried out of the way, pressing themselves against the walls and furniture; others, alerted by the noise of the scuffle, crowded in the doorways.

A lamp had been knocked off an end table, the shattered pieces littering the floor.

Hutch held a still struggling Daniel, while Cody and Jake scrambled to their feet. Tempe jumped between the combatants, her hand automatically reaching for the utility belt that was locked in the blazer.

Violet pushed her way into the room. With her hands on her hips, she said, "What on earth is going on? Jake, for goodness sake!"

"He doesn't have any right being here!" Cody

growled, glaring ferociously at Daniel.

"I've got as much right as you do," Daniel spat back. In the struggle, a lock of brown hair had escaped his pony tail, dangling in his face.

"Along with what you've done, you don't have any respect for Marella's folks."

"What is all this?" Violet asked. "What are you talking about, Cody?"

Cody smoothed his black hair with both hands. "Didn't you know that Redwing is suspected of killing your daughter?"

Again, Daniel tried pulling away from Hutch, but Hutch tightened his grip.

"Is that true?" Violet turned to Tempe for affirmation.

"Yes, but...." Tempe began. Jake lunged toward Daniel, while his wife cried, "Oh, my God! You killed my baby?"

Hutch jerked Redwing around out of Jake's path. Tempe hurled herself in front of Jake. "That's enough! Take control of yourself, you'll only make matters worse."

Jake halted with his jaw clenched, his whole body trembling. "Get him out of here...now!"

"Come on, Daniel," Hutch said, pushing him toward the open front door. The stunned gathering parted to let them through.

"Wait for me." Isabel came running through the living room, tears streaming down her face. She tucked her arm through her brother's. "I'll see that he goes home this time."

Hutch followed as far as the door to the porch. Violet touched Tempe's arm. "Deputy Crabtree, is it true? Did Daniel kill my child?"

"I don't know," Tempe said. "What I do know is that on the night of the Pow Wow, after Marella's body was taken away, Redwing ran from me."

"What do you mean?" Jake asked, his face darkened with anger. "Didn't you kick him out of the fairground earlier, like I told you?"

"Yes, I did. But he must have sneaked back in."

"Then he could have been the one who killed Marella," Jake growled.

"I told you," Cody said. "It's possible, of course. But you all need to know Redwing has been to the substation for questioning and they let him go."

"Why the hell did they do that?"

"Jake, please." Violet put her arms around her husband's waist.

"Because they didn't have enough evidence to arrest him," Tempe said.

"When will they?" Jake snapped.

She shrugged. "I don't know if they ever will...it's possible that he's not the killer. For now, I think you should forget about Daniel Redwing."

"She's right, you know," Violet said, her voice soothing. "We're surrounded by our friends, we should be receiving their offered love, not focusing on hate.

Let the deputy do her job."

Tempe thought about telling them that it wasn't up to her to find Marella's killer but knew it wouldn't help the situation. Instead, she said, "If you don't need Hutch anymore, I think we'll be going."

Violet hugged her. "Thank you for coming. And thank you, Pastor, for being here."

Hutch didn't act like he really wanted to leave, but Tempe felt they had done all they could and she wanted to make sure the Redwings had actually left the premises.

Outside, Hutch gasped, "Whew. It sure is hot!"

Tempe was glad to see Daniel's truck was gone.

"Where to now?" Hutch asked. "Obviously you have other plans."

"I want to make sure Daniel isn't hanging around somewhere. Did you smell alcohol on him?" Hutch shrugged. "Frankly, I didn't notice...but that would explain his behavior." Hutch opened the driver's side of the Blazer for her.

She climbed into the driver's seat. "I didn't smell liquor on him when he sat beside me in church, but he certainly could have drank something before he arrived at the Celsos." Tempe backed out of the parking spot and drove down the hill and out on to the road, moving slowly enough to check out any places where a truck might be tucked away. Though she did want to make sure Daniel wasn't lurking about, she had another idea.

Because Tempe knew Whitcomb's ranch butted against the reservation, it was an easy matter to locate the first private road after exiting between the river rock wall perimeter of the Indian land.

A mailbox with WHITCOMB painted on the side stood on a post near the entrance. A chain link gate blocked the way. Tempe pulled into the lane.

"Why are you stopping here?" Hutch asked, his forehead creased beneath his ruffled hair.

"As long as we're here, thought we just might call on Grant Whitcomb."

"Why?"

"Everyone seems to be forgetting that a bullet fired from his gun killed Marella."

"You don't believe his story that someone stole the gun out of his pocket?"

"It is pretty lame, don't you think?"

"Oh, I don't know. He's an old man, he might not have noticed. Do you really think he's capable of shooting someone? And why Marella?"

"What better way to get back at her father?"

Hutch sighed and got out. The lock wasn't closed, and he swung the gate open. He waited as she drove past and stopped. After closing the gate behind the Blazer, he got back in, crossing his arms and staring straight ahead.

Little more than a rough track, the lane wound up the side of a steep hill. All that was visible as they climbed was tall, dry grass.

A red-tailed hawk sat on top of one of the utility poles carrying lines to what Tempe hoped would be the residence somewhere ahead. As they drove around an outcropping of rocks, they came upon a large pond. Cattails lined the far side, algae greened the edges. One lone duck glided on the still, black surface. A tiny rowboat was tied to a rickety dock.

The peaked roof of a red barn appeared at the crest of the hill. It, along with several outbuildings, had been erected on a large, flat plateau. Behind a barbed wire fence, a few brown cattle grazed in a field. Another paved road climbed an even higher hill. What appeared to be a gray castle, complete with turrets and spires, loomed above them, perched on a pinnacle of land.

"Would you look at that?" Hutch exclaimed. "What a mansion!"

Tempe parked the Blazer next to a late model, dust-covered Ford truck. The front door opened as Tempe reached for the brass knocker on the front door. Grant Whitcomb, in his usual costume of faded plaid shirt and multi-pocketed overalls, greeted them with a gruff, "What do you want?"

A woman with a dried-apple face, wearing a ruffled apron with a bib over what used to be called a house dress, stepped in front of Whitcomb. "Shame on you, Grant. You'll have to excuse my brother's manners. Please, step inside out of the heat."

A rush of welcome cool air struck Tempe and

Hutch as they obeyed their hostess.

"I'm Alice Whitcomb. Would you like some nice lemonade and oatmeal cookies? I made them myself." The woman's eyes crinkled as her smile lifted her many wrinkles. Alice looked at least 15 years older than her sibling.

"These folks ain't here for no social call, Alice," Whitcomb growled.

Tempe offered her hand to Miss Whitcomb. "I'm Deputy Crabtree, ma'am. And this is my husband, Pastor Hutchinson."

The old woman squeezed Tempe's hand and patted it before letting go. "How do you do? I'm delighted to meet you both. We don't have many visitors." That Tempe was not in uniform didn't seem to faze her as she immediately turned her attention to Hutch. "Just where is your church, Pastor?"

Hutch grinned at her. "Bear Creek Chapel, Ma'am."

"Come along into the kitchen, both of you. I think you'll find it quite comfy in there...which is more than you can say for the rest of this house." She fixed a bright, snappy eye upon her brother before leading the way on her sturdy oxfords.

Tempe followed the bobbing white topknot around a circular staircase flanked by closed doors, down a long paneled hallway lined with more closed doors. Hutch and Mr. Whitcomb tagged behind. At the end, a final door opened into a huge room that seemed to be part kitchen, part greenhouse.

Floor to ceiling windows made up two walls. Planters spilling over with Charlies, ivies, fuchsias, and begonias hung from the ceiling. Pots and boxes arranged on the terra cotta floor held ripe tomatoes and green peppers, strawberry plants, and a variety of herbs.

"What a lovely room." Tempe admired the cupboards and walls painted the same Dutch blue as the Formica counter tops. A matching pair of arm chairs slipcovered in blue-and-white checked fabric were placed to one side. A television perched atop a cabinet nearby. An old fashioned hat tree held an assortment of hats and caps with Whitcomb's battered and stained straw hat perched on top.

"We spend all of our time here...except when we're sleeping or working outside." Miss Whitcomb went to the stainless steel refrigerator and brought out a cut glass pitcher filled with lemonade.

"This is quite a place," Hutch said.

"Please, take a seat," Miss Whitcomb said, as she placed the pitcher and four blue glasses on the round oak table in the middle of the room.

Tempe and Hutch sat in two of the straight-backed oak chairs where they could look past the plants, through the windows across a golden valley toward the mountains beyond.

Mr. Whitcomb pulled the chair opposite them away from the table a foot or two before settling himself into it.

"We call this place Grant's Folly," Alice said, smiling.

Crossing his arms, her brother snapped, "That's my sister's idea of a joke."

"Shall I pour?" Tempe asked.

"Why thank you, my dear," Miss Whitcomb said as she deposited a plate of fat, brown cookies in front of Hutch.

"Please help yourselves. Whether my brother will admit it or not, this house is pure foolishness for two old people like us. We keep most of it closed up all the time...much too expensive to heat and cool. Ridiculous waste of money building such a monstrosity."

"It was my money to waste, old woman. Provided you with ample shelter all these years. If you don't like it you can always pack up your things and move elsewhere."

It was obvious the words had been repeated so many times before that neither one listened to the other.

Tempe passed the full glasses around. "We've just come from Marella Celso's funeral."

"Such a shame," Miss Whitcomb said. "I read about it in the paper. It must be terribly hard on the family. Such nice people.

"Don't be such a hypocrite, Alice. The Deputy knows all about the trouble them daggone savages been causing us over the years."

Lifting her sagging chin, she delivered a murderous glance toward her brother. "Just because you've never been able to get along with our neighbors, don't include me in your silly feud. I've always told you, if you'd just treat those folks with some common decency they wouldn't get such joy out of bedeviling you all the time."

"Shows how little you know. They ain't got sense enough to know what common decency is."

"You are positively hopeless, Grant Whitcomb."

Tempe sipped her lemonade and nibbled on a cookie, as she listened to Mr. Whitcomb and his sister. "Did your brother tell you that his gun was used to kill Marella?"

Miss Whitcomb's mouth dropped open and she gasped. "Oh, good Lord, Grant, no! Surely you didn't..."

"Hush your mouth, woman! What's the matter with you. You know I wouldn't kill no one."

"You threatened to often enough."

"Stop it! You want the deputy to arrest me? Then where would you be? Who'd do the work around here? How would you pay the bills?" Whitcomb glared at his sister.

Turning to face Tempe, he said, "I didn't shoot that girl. It's true that I don't have no use for her father. Indians been coming over here, stealing my cattle and setting fires on my land for years. Jake always stands up for them, even when I've darn near caught the culprit red-handed. He's nothing but a smooth-talking crook with some kind of pull with the law. Always manages to weasel out of everything."

The description didn't sound like the Jake Celso Tempe knew. Though hot-tempered, he seemed fair-minded and honest. That he'd have any unusual influence on the law was doubtful. Tempe glanced at her husband who lifted one of his auburn eyebrows.

"I still find it difficult to believe that someone managed to steal your gun out of your pocket without you noticing," Tempe said.

"Is that what he says happened?" Miss Whitcomb began to chuckle.

"I told you to hush your mouth, woman."

When she'd contained herself, Alice added, "As outlandish as that sounds, I wouldn't doubt it a bit."

"Why do you say that?" Hutch asked.

"Sometimes my brother doesn't even know where he is, much less what's going on around him. I see him standing out in the field, staring off into space. When he's like that, I suspect someone could empty all his pockets without him knowing it. Mr. Whitcomb scooted around in his chair so he was no longer facing the table. "You didn't have to say that. Makes me sound like some kind of old fool."

A smile lifted his sister's lips.

"If someone did steal the gun from you prior to Marella's death, it takes you off the list of suspects," Tempe said.

"Seems like I ought to be hearing a great big thank

you," Miss Whitcomb said.

"Not likely," her brother grumbled. "Is there anything else you want to ask me, Deputy? It's time I got back to work."

When they were headed back down the narrow, winding track through the fields of dry grass, Hutch said, "Guess you can forget about Mr. Whitcomb. His sister certainly helped with his alibi."

"Maybe, maybe not. She could have made that bit up about him spacing out in order to help him."

"I doubt it. The way they sparred with each other, it didn't sound like she'd give him that kind of help."

"I'm not sure about that. Despite all the nasty cracks back and forth, he lets her live in his house, she keeps it spotless for him and cooks his meals. Besides, I think they enjoy needling each other."

As soon as they arrived home, Tempe dialed the sub-station and asked for Sergeant Guthrie. Hutch rolled his eyes but Tempe ignored him.

"Deputy Crabtree here. Did you get the results of the Celso autopsy yet?" She knew he had, since the body had been released for the funeral.

"The Celso investigation is not part of your job, Crabtree," the sergeant said. She could hear papers rustling.

"I know that, Sergeant. I'm curious. Was there anything interesting or out of the ordinary?"

"As a matter of fact, Crabtree, there was." He paused.

She waited impatiently for him to go on, afraid if she asked for the information, he'd just tell her it wasn't any of her business.

"There was no sign of rape or recent sexual activity. However, Marella Celso was pregnant."

12

"Oh, my." Tempe replaced the phone.

"What was that all about?" Hutch asked, as he draped his suit jacket over a kitchen chair.

"Marella was pregnant."

Hutch's face expressed the surprise Tempe had felt upon hearing the news. "Well, well, well. Cody's, I imagine."

"Seems logical," Tempe said. "But Isabel Redwing told me today that Marella had broken her engagement with Cody. Why would she do that if she knew she was pregnant with his child?"

"Maybe Isabel thinks inventing trouble between Marella and Cody will somehow protect her brother. What are we going to do about dinner?"

"I don't know. I hadn't even thought about it. Since we're all dressed up we ought to go out. The couple were certainly having some sort of a problem at the Pow Wow, the only time I saw them together. But all romances have their ups and downs."

"True. Why don't we go to the Inn? We haven't been there in a while."

"I'd like that." Tempe's mind was still on the murder. "It's hard to figure out who is telling the truth. Isabel may be protecting Daniel, Alice Whitcomb lying to cover up for her brother, and we probably haven't heard the truth from Redwing, Endrezza or Whitcomb either. And I haven't been able to get Katherine Davelos to say much of anything."

"Oh, dear, what about Blair? He probably won't be interested in eating at the Inn."

Hutch gazed out the window. "He's pulling into the driveway right now. We'll ask him."

The invitation was unnecessary because Blair came into the house munching on a hamburger. "They fed us at the Cafe after the fire, and we have a training meeting at the station in a little while."

Tempe kissed her son absently. "We're going to the Inn for dinner."

"Good. You two need some time alone."

"And it'll give me a chance to ask Two John some questions I've been wondering about," Tempe said.

Hutch shook his head, and Blair scolded, "Mother!"

* * *

The Bear Creek Inn had once been a stage coach stop. Over the years it had been added onto, turned into a hotel in the thirties, and remodeled into a restaurant and lodge in the late seventies. Of stacked-log construction, the building retained its historic atmosphere.

Hutch and Tempe were greeted just inside the entrance by Claudia Donato, the owner of the Inn, as she stepped from behind a high desk. As always, Claudia's shoulder-length blonde hair had been arranged in the latest style and she wore a simple light blue dress that Tempe knew was far more expensive than it looked.

Her smile was genuine as she said, "How nice to see you both. It's been a while."

Tempe was embarrassed when she realized it had been since the wedding reception which had been held at the Inn. "Yes, it has. And I must thank you again for the lovely party you gave us."

"And I echo those sentiments. We'll both remember it always," Hutch added. Unfortunately they probably wouldn't remember the occasion because of how nice it was. Everyone in Bear Creek had attended, not only to offer congratulations to the newlyweds but it was also an opportunity to sample the Inn's cuisine and drink without having to pay for it. Tempe and Hutch had stayed only as long as they felt appropriate to show their appreciation for all of Claudia's work. Blair reported later that the party had continued far into the evening.

They paid the bill after returning from their honeymoon. The honeymoon might not have been quite so blissful if they had known how much the reception was going to cost.

In order to economize, they'd since limited their meals out to the far cheaper Cafe.

"You both look as though marriage is agreeing with you," Claudia said as she led them into the dining room.

Hutch hugged Tempe as they followed Claudia into the cavernous room which was dominated by the original stone fireplace that comprised the end wall. The worn, hardwood floors gleamed with polish. Long, pale blue linen cloths covered the round tables. A single rose in a crystal vase decorated each one.

"Is this all right?" Claudia put two menus on a secluded table near the far window. They could watch the traffic traveling up and down the highway.

"Perfect," Tempe said. "Is Nick here tonight?"

"Surprisingly enough, he is. While he was working on the Pow Wow he left at sunrise and didn't return until long after the customers had gone home. But he promised to make it up to me and he's supervising the kitchen tonight."

"When he has some free time, I'd like to see him," Tempe said.

"I'll tell him you're out here. I know he'll want to say hello to both of you. A waitress will be with you shortly." Before Claudia returned to her post behind the desk, she opened one of the swinging doors leading to the kitchen and poked her head inside.

As Tempe and Hutch were examining the menu, Nick Two John appeared beside their table. His long braids hung down the back of the white shirt he wore tucked into his faded Levis. "Claudia said you wanted to see me."

"Your menu has changed since we were here last," Hutch said. "Any suggestions?"

The handsome Indian's expression didn't change, though Tempe was sure that he knew he hadn't been requested to come out of the kitchen to make a recommendation about their dinner choice.

"Since I took over supervising the kitchen, I thought we ought to go back to more basic food items."

"Venison, buffalo, trout...frog legs? That's basic?" Tempe questioned.

Still with no change of expression, Two John said, "Basic to our people."

"The frog legs interest me," Tempe said.

"The meat is much like chicken with a slightly fishy taste."

"I'm sticking to beef," Hutch said.

"I'll send the waitress." Two John started to leave.

"Can you stay for a minute?" Tempe asked. "I wanted to talk to you about something."

Two John crossed his arms. "To do with Marella's murder."

"Yes. There's a question about what happened to Marella's ticket money. There was no money on her body. But shouldn't there have been some? Every time I saw her she was selling tickets."

Interest sparked in his dark eyes. "Of course she

turned money and ticket stubs in periodically. We kept a running count of the stubs. From the beginning we knew Marella had sold far more tickets than any of the other Princess contestants."

Hutch leaned forward. "What if someone killed Marella for the ticket money? It could have been a stranger tempted by the wad of bills she carried."

"That's a possibility of course. But why weren't there any stubs? They were gone too. No reason for anyone to steal those," Tempe said.

A frown furrowed Nick's bronze forehead. "I remember something. A few minutes before it was time for the Princess to be named, Katherine Davelos deposited some money in the cash box but she didn't put any stubs into her daughter's container. I thought it was kind of odd at the time but things got pretty hectic right about then."

Excited, Tempe said, "Tell me how that worked when the girls turned their money and stubs in."

"It's real simple. There was one cash box for all the money, but each girl had her own container for stubs. From time to time we counted them and put a rubber band around those, keeping a running total for each contestant. A girl usually turned in her money and her stubs at the same time."

"Maybe Katherine killed Marella and scooped up the money and her stubs. She might have thrown the stubs away so Marella wouldn't get the credit. Not wanting to be a thief, she turned in the cash," Tempe theorized.

"Katherine certainly had no love for Marella," Nick said. "She a strange one. The worst kind of Wannabee."

Hutch wrinkled his brow. "Wannabee?"

"There're four kinds of Indians...Traditional, Pow Wow, Born Again, and Wannabee."

"I didn't think Katherine had any Indian blood," Hutch said.

"No, but she sure wishes she did...Wannabee an Indian."

Hutch nodded. "Explain the other categories, Nick."

"Traditional is an Indian who remains true to the old ways. A Pow Wow Indian is one whose whole life is caught up in going to Pow Wows. And Born Agains you ought to be the most familiar with, Pastor. They're the ones like the Celsos. Indians who mix Christianity with their Indian beliefs."

Hutch grinned. "My kind of folks."

Two John remained stoic. "I don't care much for Katherine, but it is difficult to imagine her shooting Marella."

"Maybe she didn't do it herself," Tempe said. "Perhaps she hired someone to do her dirty work."

"Like the woman who hired a hit man to kill the mother of her daughter's cheerleading rival," Hutch put in.

"I wouldn't put it past her, but if that's what she

did, how do you go about finding out who did it?"
Two John asked.

Tempe shrugged. "It isn't up to me to even specu-
late about it."

"But she can't help herself." Hutch lifted Tempe's
hand to his mouth and kissed it. "That's one of my
wife's many endearing qualities."

"One of my faults is what he really means," Tempe
said.

Nick bowed his head briefly, and Tempe thought
he was hiding a smile. But when he raised his head
again, his expression was as impassive as usual. "Enjoy your evening."

They did. Tempe bravely tried the frog legs, finding them delicious as long as she avoided looking at
the tiny, webbed feet on the ends. Though they hadn't
made a spoken agreement, neither she nor Hutch mentioned Marella's murder again during the remainder
of their evening out.

* * *

The next day as Tempe went about her regular
working day routine, she couldn't control the questions that kept popping into her head. After Blair left
for school and Hutch went off to make a pastoral call,
Tempe began a load of laundry before launching herself on her usual jog around the neighborhood.

Tempe didn't notice the oak, aspen or pines covering the hillsides, nor the tumble-down appearance
of the old cemetery where her pioneer ancestors were

buried. She jogged past a boulder-strewn pasture, the cattle lifting their heads to stare at her passing. Picking up speed, she pushed herself as she ran over the crest of a hill and down the other side.

A pair of Great Blue Herons flew overhead, squawking their displeasure at being disturbed, casting their prehistoric-appearing shadows on the road in front of her. As her L.A. Gears pounded the pavement, her mind tumbled thoughts about Marella's murder. If Katherine Davelos hadn't killed Marella, what was she doing over in the area near the body just before Tempe discovered it? Did she just stumble upon Marella's corpse by accident? Not likely, since it was out of the way of the Pow Wow activities.

Maybe she did hire a hit man and was just checking to make sure he'd done the job. And while she was there, scooped up the cash hoping it would be assumed the motive for murder was robbery, taking the stubs too so that they wouldn't be counted for Marella.

Katherine certainly acted like she had something to hide when Tempe tried to question her, but then again, she had a nasty personality and acted like that under most circumstances. But if given the opportunity, Tempe would like to ask her about the tickets and the money in order to see if she could get any kind of reaction out of her.

Tempe jogged past an old farm house that had once belonged to a great aunt and uncle Tempe barely remembered. Aunt Lily had been round, smelled like lavender, and made wonderful crisp gingersnaps. Uncle Bill smoked a pipe and told stories about when he worked for a logging camp high in the Sierra, bringing overloaded wagons full of logs down the steep mountain roads. They had long since passed away, their offspring moving to more prosperous parts of California. Tempe and Blair were the only ones left in Bear Creek.

Thinking about the old relatives brought Grant Whitcomb to mind. The ornery rancher certainly had enough hatred in his heart to shoot Marella. It made no difference to him what kind of girl Marella was--that she belonged to Jake Celso and was an Indian could be motive enough.

Meeting his sister hadn't changed Tempe's assessment of Whitcomb. And then there were the young people.

Tempe made her turn and headed back the way she came. It was going to be another hot day. Perspiration beaded on her forehead as heat shimmered up from the pavement in waves. She wished she had time to go back to the reservation. Tempe would like to ask Isabel if she knew her friend was pregnant. And what about Daniel? Could he have heard Marella confiding in his sister about her news? Did Cody know he was going to be a father? Was it his? But if he hadn't made Marella pregnant, who had?

Unfortunately she might never find out the answers

to her questions.

An enormous crow, its feathers ragged, peered down at her from its perch atop a woodpecker-riddled telephone pole. Sounding as though it mocked her dilemma, the bird cawed.

13

After lunch, Tempe headed toward Dennison. Hutch asked her to do some banking for him while he visited a sick church member. Though she would rather have stayed home, she hoped doing her husband's errand might ease some of the annoyance he felt about her preoccupation with the murder.

As she approached the entrance to the lake, a small truck turned in front of her, four bare-chested young men perched along the sides of the bed hooted and hollered. She slammed on her brakes to keep from hitting the vehicle. Because the truck was going far too fast to maneuver the turn easily, the tires squealed as it swerved on the narrow road. Those in the back didn't seem particularly upset as they clung tightly to keep from being thrown from their precarious perch.

Tempe suspected they'd been drinking. She wasn't wearing her uniform nor was she officially on duty, but she followed the truck. The driver of the truck didn't seem to notice the official vehicle behind him because he didn't slow down.

The truck bounced over a speed bump, jostling the passengers in the bed -- and again they hollered.

Tempe switched on her overhead light bar. The driver ignored it.

The truck speeded up as it entered the large parking lot next to the lake. The lot was half filled with cars. A man in a bathing suit dodged out of the way to keep from being struck by the vehicle as it raced toward the boat loading ramp.

"Oh no!" Tempe cried out and turned on her siren knowing nothing could stop the inevitable. An older model Buick laboriously hauled a trailer carrying a speed boat straight into the path of the truck.

Brakes squealed, someone screamed, the passengers in the bed yelled and bailed out from both sides onto the pavement, fleeing in all directions. The truck struck the boat and trailer. Tempe heard the loud crash, followed by the sound of wood splintering. As it shoved the boat and trailer in a wide arc, the truck finally came to a halt at a right angle to the Buick.

Tempe used the Bronco's radio to report the accident and request assistance. The driver of the Buick burst out of the car, a heavy-set man, his face flushed with anger.

"What the Sam Hill is going on? You blind or something?"

Before Tempe could climb out of her vehicle, the door on the driver's side of the truck banged open and a skinny, teenager wearing only cut-offs and a base-ball cap took off on bare feet toward the lake.

Tempe started after him with the fat boat owner puffing along behind.

"What is this...you a deputy or something...get my hands on that son-of-a gun..."

Quickly outdistancing her pursuer, Tempe could no longer hear him. The escaping youth trampled through the middle of a picnic spread out on a blanket, scattering plates of food and knocking over soda cans. Angry shouts greeted Tempe as she darted around the picnickers.

Beginning to wonder if she was going to be able to catch up with the young man, Tempe saw him headed toward an old man nodding lazily behind a propped fishing pole. Just as one bare foot smacked down in front of the fisherman, a skinny arm snared the runner's calf.

It was enough to upset his balance, and he fell heavily onto his hands and knees. Before he could pull himself upright, Tempe pounced on top of him. "Hold it right there."

With her knee in the middle of his back, Tempe began her recitation. "You have the right to...."

When she'd finished she yanked him to his feet. No more than eighteen, the sullen youth glared at her with bloodshot eyes. His beery breath came at her in waves.

"Good tackle," the old fisherman cackled. The

boy cast a murderous glance in his direction. Unfazed, the old man returned his attention to the unmoving line trailing off from his pole into the lake.

Because she was off duty and dressed in her at-home outfit of shorts and T-shirt, Tempe didn't have any handcuffs. She hung onto the young man's arm and led him back up the sloping bank toward the parking lot. A highway patrol car was parked near her Blazer and one of the lake patrol trucks had pulled in front of the Buick. The two uniformed men stared at her as she approached.

From the corner of her eye, Tempe noticed someone else watching her. A woman in a bikini lying on a beach towel, with her head propped on her hands. Oversized dark glasses hid her eyes. A straw hat covered most of her hair though some of the dyed black locks could be seen. Tempe knew it was Katherine Davelos.

"Here," Tempe said, pushing the youth toward the highway patrolman. "I'm not on duty. Take over. Drunk driving, resisting arrest, etc."

With a jerk of his head toward the still-sputtering boat owner, the highway patrolman said, "The victim says you were a witness to the accident."

"That's right. Followed the kid because he was driving recklessly and at an unsafe speed. He ignored my signal to pull over and drove right into that boat and trailer. I'll see that you get my written report." Tempe glanced back at where she spotted Katherine and saw the woman was on her feet headed toward the far end of the parking lot.

"I've got to go." Without waiting for permission, Tempe galloped after Katherine.

With her towel draped over her shoulders and fluttering at her sides, Katherine strode purposefully toward her yellow Mustang parked beneath the overhanging branches of an oak tree. Her plump behind swung in the skimpy bikini bottom, her muscled legs glistening from a recent oiling.

When Tempe had almost caught up to the woman, she called out, "Mrs. Davelos...Katherine...wait. I'd like to talk with you."

Katherine halted and turned around. She lowered her dark glasses enough so that Tempe could see her blue eyes.

"I don't have anything to say to you, Deputy Crabtree." Katherine seemed much shorter than she had before, but Tempe realized it was because of she had on flat-soled sandals instead of the high heels she'd worn before.

"Oh, I think you do. I heard you make the prediction that someone was going to die the day of the Pow Wow. Were you planning Marella's murder at that time?"

Katherine's red lips dropped open. "I can't believe you said that. Are you accusing me of murder?"

Tempe realized she might have gone too far but it was all she could think of that would make Katherine talk to her. "No, I'm not accusing you of anything. But there are a few questions I'd like to ask."

Katherine sighed and glanced at her watch. "Is this going to take very long?"

"Not if you answer my questions truthfully."

"Look, I came up here to the lake to work on my tan. I don't want to waste my time. Let me soak up a few more rays while you're doing whatever it is you think you have to do."

Katherine didn't wait for agreement from Tempe. She spread out her towel on a bit of scraggly grass in front of her car and dropped down on it, stretching out her shapely legs.

Not wanting to turn any browner than she already was, Tempe lowered herself into a cross-legged position in the shade of the large tree. "Tell me about your prediction."

"If you knew anything at all about Indian tradition, you'd realize that a dog howling at night always means that someone is soon to die. I heard the dog howling...Marella died and that's all there is to it."

"You had nothing to do with Marella's death?"

"Of course not. I'm not a murderer."

"Last night my husband and I went out to dinner...."

Katherine interrupted. "Very nice for you I'm sure, but what does that have to do with...."

"We talked to Nick Two John while we were there. He said you brought some ticket money in and deposited it right before the identity of the Princess was announced, but you didn't turn in any stubs. That seems very strange. If that was your daughter's ticket money you'd have been sure to turn in the stubs. Where did you get the money, Mrs. Davelos?" Scrambling to her feet, Katherine snatched up her towel. "I'm not talking to you any more, Deputy Crabtree. If the detectives want to know something else they can contact me directly." She marched toward her car and yanked open the door.

"Why won't you tell me, Katherine? Do you have something to hide?" Tempe called as the woman fired up her engine and backed out of the parking space.

Tempe returned to her Blazer.

"Don't forget that report," the highway patrolman hollered.

* * *

By the time she'd finished verbally describing what she'd seen, and writing it all out, it was too late to go to the bank. When she neared their cottage, she saw Hutch's old blue and white truck and felt guilty because she hadn't taken care of his errand. With bank bag in hand, she entered the house. Hutch was at the sink washing salad greens.

"Hi sweetie." She greeted him with a kiss.

His smile faded when he spotted the bulging bank bag in her hand.

"I'm afraid I didn't make it to the bank. I'll go tomorrow, I promise."

His forehead furrowed. "What happened? Trouble

with the Blazer?"

"No, nothing like that. I had to work an accident."

She had already made up her mind not to say any-thing about running into Katherine Davelos.

"But you aren't on duty yet." His tone betrayed his irritation.

"That doesn't matter when I see something hap-pening. It's the same with any law enforcement of-ficer. A bunch of kids were driving recklessly right in front of me. They had an accident and I had no choice but to arrest the driver. Highway patrol took over but I still had to file a written report about what I saw."

Hutch nodded. "I understand." But his expres-sion contradicted his words.

He circled her with his arms. "It seems like there's never any time for us."

Tempe forgot the murder and her job for a mo-ment as she relaxed in her husband's embrace. She pressed her cheek against his, inhaling his fresh, clean scent. "I love you."

Hutch kissed her deeply and she felt the stirring of her passion for him. If only it wasn't time for her to get ready for work.

Reluctantly she stepped away from him. Tapping her watch, she said, "Sorry."

Hutch sighed with unhappy resignation. She could feel him staring after her as she headed toward their bedroom. While she showered and put on her uni-form she wondered where Blair was, and felt ashamed that it had taken so long for concern about her son to even pop into her mind. Maybe Hutch was right, maybe her job and Marella's murder had taken on far more importance that it should.

But she'd barely mulled that thought over when another popped in unbidden. She wanted to talk to Isabel again, find out if she knew Marella was pregnant and by whom. Somehow she'd figure out a way to go to the reservation again to see Isabel.

Blair was in the kitchen with Hutch when she came out. He sat on his tailbone with his long legs stretched out under the table, his hands behind his head. He looked tired and smelled of smoke.

She leaned down and kissed his forehead. "Hi, honey. Where have you been?"

"Fire up on Poppy's Peak."

"Seems like there's been an awful lot of fires lately," Tempe said.

"It's the season," Blair said.

"Time for me to go to work." Tempe glanced at Hutch who seemed unusually quiet. He nodded his head but his expression was grim.

Blair glanced from his mother to Hutch and back again.

He sat up straight. "Honeymoon over?"

"I wouldn't say that." Tempe couldn't help wondering if her son might be right.

"Something's wrong," Blair said, fixing his gaze on Hutch as though expecting an explanation.

Hutch shrugged and jammed his hands in his pockets. "Just feeling neglected, I guess."

Blair grinned. "Seems like I spent most of my life that way. You get used to it after awhile. Doesn't mean she loves you any less."

"Hey," Tempe interjected. "You're talking about me like I'm not here."

"That's because you aren't most of the time," Hutch said.

"Wait a minute, that's not fair! I warned you about my job before we ever got married." Anger bubbled inside her.

"It's not your job. I can handle the job. You aren't here even when you are."

Blair nodded toward his mother in agreement with Hutch. "Yep, he's got that right."

"Lately when you're home, you're always thinking about Marella Celso's murder."

Hutch's accusation was valid. That's what she did. But she couldn't help herself. "I'm sorry it bothers you both so much. But I don't know how to stop."

"Easy. Think about Blair and me when you're home."

Blair laughed. "You're asking the impossible."

Tempe felt like they were ganging up on her and she didn't like it. "I'm going to be late for work. You two have a good time complaining about me while I'm gone!"

She snatched open the door and started out. Hutch

came after her and put a hand on her shoulder. "I don't want you to go away angry."

"Then you shouldn't have started a fight with me when I have to go to work."

He gently turned her around until she faced him. "I didn't mean for us to argue. It just seems very strange to miss someone when they're in the same room with you. I love you, Tempe. I married you because I want us to share our lives...and I feel shut out of yours."

She didn't have the time it would take to resolve the problem. "I love you too, Hutch. I don't like it when we argue but I have to go now." She kissed him lightly on the lips and headed for the Blazer.

He was still standing in the doorway watching after her when she drove around the corner heading for the highway.

Fortunately, she was busy the entire evening investigating reported gun shots, a stolen pick-up, a house burglary, stopping a bar fight and taking the drunken participants home, and making several traffic stops. There was no time to consider her problem with Hutch or Marella's murder.

By the time she was off work, both Hutch and Blair were asleep. When she slipped under the sheet beside Hutch he took her in his arms without waking.

* * *

The harsh sound of the phone ringing awakened her in the morning. Hutch didn't answer it. When she picked up the receiver, Sergeant Guthrie's voice blasted in her ear.

"Crabtree, I want to see you just as soon as you can get here."

14

Neither Hutch nor Blair were in the house. She found a note on the kitchen table from Hutch. He had gone to Dennison to take care of the banking himself and planned to shop for groceries while he was there. Blair had gone to the fire station. Tempe was glad she didn't have to face a continuation of last night's argument.

That Hutch was still angry was obvious since he'd gone off without waking her. There wasn't even any coffee left for her in the pot. He'd washed it and it set upside down in the dish drainer.

She decided to stop in the cafe for a cup of coffee to take with her.

When she stepped in the sergeant's office she was surprised to see Detective Morrison. He leaned back in the chair until he saw her, then he jumped to his feet. Bending until his lopsided nose nearly touched hers, he shouted, "What the hell do you think you're doing, Crabtree?" A fine spray of saliva struck her and she could smell coffee and mints on his breath.

"Cool it, Morrison," Sergeant Guthrie warned from behind his desk. "I'll handle this, she's one of my people."

Tempe couldn't imagine what this was all about. It was unusual to see Morrison without Richards; she couldn't think of another time when they weren't a pair.

"Sit down, Crabtree," Guthrie said, gruffly. "You too, Morrison."

The detective glowered at the sergeant but did as he was told. Tempe perched uneasily on the edge of the folding chair. "What's the problem?"

"You been messing in our case again," Morrison said.

"Morrison," Guthrie snapped. "We've had a complaint about you, Crabtree."

"What kind of complaint?" She ought to be getting used to this by now. It seemed everyone had something against her.

"Harassment."

"Harassment? Who am I supposed to have harassed." Though she acted surprised she had a pretty good idea who the complaint had come from.

The sergeant glanced at the yellow pad in front of him. "Katherine Davelos. Says you accosted her at the lake. Badgered her with questions. Accused her of murdering the Celso girl."

"Accosted? Badgered? Accused? Really, don't

you think I know better than that?"

"Are you telling us that you didn't talk to Mrs. Davelos yesterday?" Morrison asked.

"Oh, I talked to her all right but I didn't accost, badger, and accuse. All I did was ask her a few questions." Tempe tried to sound as unconcerned as possible to cover up the uneasiness she felt.

"But you aren't supposed to be talking to anyone about the murder, Crabtree, it isn't your job!" Morrison exploded.

"But you haven't been asking the right question," Tempe said quietly.

"How do you know what questions we've been asking?" Morrison's ugly face had turned a plum color.

Still keeping her voice calm, Tempe queried, "Have you talked to Katherine Davelos about the prediction she made that someone would die on the day of the Pow Wow? Or did you ask her how she happened to have Marella's money? Or what she did with the ticket stubs?"

"I don't know what the hell you're talking about!" Morrison crossed his big arms over his massive chest.

"What are you talking about, Crabtree?" Guthrie's bushy graying brows nearly came together over his deep set eyes.

"I overheard Mrs. Davelos telling Marella's mother that a dog howled all night which meant someone would die."

Morrison made a rude snorting noise.

"Go on," Guthrie prompted.

"Mrs. Davelos did not get along with Mrs. Celso. She wanted her own daughter to win the Princess contest so badly she pushed the poor girl unmercifully to sell her tickets."

"You think Katherine Davelos killed Marella Celso to help her daughter win the contest?" Guthrie asked.

"She's all wet," Morrison interjected. "The Davelos woman is too short...only stands five-foot-two--same as the Celso girl. Whoever fired the fatal shot had to be taller." The detective looked smug.

"You didn't pay enough attention to Mrs. Davelos that night, Detective, or you would have noticed that she was wearing high-heeled boots which made her several inches taller than the victim." Tempe had known all along that the detectives had been so sure Daniel Redwing was the murderer that they hadn't taken enough time with any of the other possible suspects or evidence. Maybe this would make them be more conscientious with their investigation.

"Are you sure about that?" Sergeant Guthrie asked, frowning even more.

"Of course, I am. I saw Mrs. Davelos off and on all that day and evening. Her boots were leather with fringed cuffs...and four inch heels."

The plum color changed to an even deeper purple. Morrison hauled a small notebook out of his jacket pocket. He flipped a few pages and scribbled something. "Okay. What's all this about money and ticket stubs?"

"Sergeant, didn't you ask him?"

"I told you Crabtree said you needed to check on that, remember?" Sergeant Guthrie's normal ruddiness had deepened also.

"Yeah, yeah. It didn't seem important at the time. You've got my attention now, Crabtree."

Tempe was beginning to enjoy herself. The situation had reversed, with Detective Morrison being on the hot seat instead of her. "Marella was the actual winner of the Princess contest because she sold the most tickets. Every time I saw her she was making a sale. She should have had money and ticket stubs with her."

"Didn't find neither on the body."   "Doesn't it make you wonder what happened to them? Maybe the murderer stole the money. But why would anyone steal the stubs? Only someone who wanted to make sure that Marella's didn't get counted. And that points to Mrs. Davelos."

"Maybe. But what about her daughter and the other contestants?" the Sergeant asked.

"Linda Davelos didn't even want to be in the contest. The other two girls' mothers didn't make noticeable appearances. Those girls just seemed to be enjoying themselves. One of them, Isabel Redwing, was Marella's best friend."

Morrison leaned closer to Tempe. "Isabel Redwing? Any connection to Daniel?"

Tempe found it hard to believe it had been four days since the murder and the detectives hadn't found out any of that information. "She's his sister." Taking a deep breath, Tempe plunged ahead with an idea she had. All the sergeant and the detective could do was say no. "I spoke with Isabel briefly after Marella's funeral."

"Yeah, Guthrie told me you were going." Morrison seemed torn between being irritated at Tempe and eager to hear what she had to say. "Find out anything important?"

"Only that Marella had broken up with Cody Endrezza...even though he certainly hasn't shared that information with anyone."

"The Sergeant tell you that Marella was pregnant?"

Tempe nodded. "Isabel is the only one who might know for sure who the father was. I'd like to talk to Isabel some more."

Morrison scooted his chair further away from her. "It's not your job to interview murder witnesses or suspects."

"I'm well aware of that fact, Detective, you've certainly reminded me often enough. But I don't think Isabel will be candid with you or Richards. She's very protective of her brother and the confidences she shared with Marella. But I might be able to get her to open up to me. I'd like permission to try." Tempe held her breath while Morrison and the Sergeant exchanged glances.

"Sounds good to me," Guthrie said.

"Richards isn't going to be happy about this but I got a gut level feeling you might have something. Okay, go ahead and take a shot at it. Give me a call as soon as you find out something." He narrowed his eyes. "But don't go poking your nose in anywhere else, got that?"

Tempe had to fight to keep from smiling. "Yes, sir."

"That means staying away from Katherine Davelos and anyone else you might run into on the reservation," Sergeant Guthrie warned.

"Yes sir."

"So when do you think you'll be going out there?" Morrison asked.

"Since I'm in uniform, I suppose right now is as good a time as any. Of course, there's no guarantee that I'll find her at home. I don't even know where she lives."

After flipping back through his notebook, Morrison rattled off an address.

* * *

Tempe drove toward the reservation, her mind full of her good fortune of actually being sent to talk to Isabel by Detective Morrison. Even if she hadn't been given permission, she knew that she would have figured out some way to talk to Isabel no matter who it upset--the Sergeant, Detective Morrison, even Hutch.

She found the Redwing's place at the end of a winding dirt lane off one of the many side roads deep in the reservation. It was an ancient, battered single-wide mobile home set upon a foundation of cement blocks. Dust dulled the orange paint of an older model Datsun parked in front. A chicken wire fence surrounded an attempt at a garden. Scraggly marigolds poked their bright heads between the tomato plants. Despite the proliferation of weeds and the lack of water, Tempe spotted several plump, bright red fruit peeking out through the sun-scorched leaves.

After parking the Blazer beside the Datsun, Tempe climbed the rickety, unpainted wooden stairs leading to a tiny porch no longer attached to the metal building. First she pushed the bell, but when she didn't hear anything, she knocked on the door.

A curtain at the nearest window was pulled aside momentarily. Tempe heard the floor creak as someone approached.

The door opened a crack and Isabel peeked out. "What do you want?"

Tempe knew her uniform made the teenager suspicious.

"I just want to talk to you a little more, Isabel. May I come in?"

"My mother's sleeping. She works nights at the hospital."

"We can talk quietly."

With obvious reluctance, Isabel stepped back, opening the door for Tempe.

A swamp cooler labored noisily, affording a damp draftiness to the narrow living room. Though the furniture sagged and the upholstery was worn, everything was neat and clean. The linoleum had been mopped so often the pattern had nearly disappeared. The kitchen and dining area were at the front end of the trailer and had the same tidy order though the vinyl on the chairs had been patched with duct tape, and the cupboards' finish had been dulled by countless scrubbing.

Tempe glanced the other way and saw a hallway leading to the closed doors of bedrooms.

"You might as well sit down, Deputy," Isabel said.

Tempe settled at the end of the couch. Isabel stood staring at her, nervously tucking her Madras shirt into the waistline of her cutoffs as she shifted on her bare feet.

"Is this going to take very long? I have jobs I'm supposed to do for my mother."

"Relax, Isabel. I just want to ask you a few questions."

"I told you everything there was after Marella's funeral." Isabel leaned against the wooden arm of an over-stuffed chair with a lumpy cushion, crossing her arms and her feet at the ankles.

"Where's your brother?"

Isabel lowered her eyes for a moment before answering. "He would have been at work now if it hadn't been for you."

"What do you mean?"

"He had a job in town until yesterday."

"What happened?"

"His boss was at the funeral. He found out that Danny was a suspect. He called yesterday morning and fired him...just like that. He didn't even give Danny a chance to explain." Tears filled Isabel's eyes. "Mom doesn't know any of this yet. It's gonna kill her when she finds out people think Danny murdered Marella."

"All the more reason for you to talk to me, Isabel. You may know something that will help us find out who the real murderer is."

"If I knew, don't you think I'd tell you? I love my brother. I don't want him to go to jail for something he didn't do. That's one thing I do know. Danny didn't kill Marella. He wouldn't have hurt her for anything." Isabel pushed her hair away from her face.

"Where's your father?" Tempe asked.

"Who knows? He was a drunk. Might be dead. Left my mom when we were little kids. She raised us all by herself." Isabel lifted her head proudly. "She's an LVN. Never had any help from anyone."

"Yesterday I asked you about Marella's relationship with Cody and you said she'd broken up with him. But you wouldn't tell me what caused the break-up."

"And I'm not going to." Isabel pressed her lips together tightly.

"I think it may be important to the case. It might have something to do with why she was killed."

"I can't tell you. Marella made me promise not to tell anyone." The tears that had been threatening spilled from Isabel's eyes. "It's the only thing left that I can do for her."

"No, Isabel, there is something more. Isabel wiped her damp cheek with the back of her hand. "Like what?"

"Help me find out who killed her."

"How many times do I have to say it? Don't you think if I knew who did it I would tell you? I don't know!"

"Don't you see, if you'll be open with me about Marella, share all the things she's told you, maybe together we can figure out who did it."

Isabel shook her head.

Tempe had saved the most important question last. "Did you know Marella was pregnant?"

Isabel gasped. "How did you find out?"

15

"Whenever there's a murder, an autopsy must be done on the victim's body," Tempe said.

"Oh, my God! They cut her up?" Isabel cried.

"She wasn't there to feel anything."

"Do her parents know?"

"Oh yes. They were told that an autopsy had to be done before the body could be released to them for the funeral."

"No, no." Isabel waved her hand as though to dispel Tempe's answer. "I meant do they know that Marella was pregnant?"

"I'm not sure. I doubt if they knew the day of the funeral or Mrs. Celso would have mentioned it to me. But eventually someone will tell them, I'm sure."

"Why do they ever have to find out? Marella didn't want them to know."

"Unless she planned to have an abortion, they would have found out sooner or later."

"Marella would never have had an abortion. But

she hadn't made up her mind what she was going to do. She'd been thinking about all sorts of things. Maybe going to some big city to have the baby...maybe adopting it out. Lots of people want babies. She might have kept it."

"Did she consider marrying the father?" Tempe asked.

Before Isabel could answer, the front door burst open. "What do you think you're doing?" Daniel slammed the door shut. Swaying, he stared at Tempe with open hostility. He was obviously drunk.

Tempe stood. "I've been talking to your sister, Daniel."

"I want you to get out of here, now!"

"Please, Daniel, don't wake Mom." Isabel took hold of her brother's arm.

"Let go of me." He shrugged away from her. "Are you leaving or do I have to help you out?" His alcoholic breath came in waves toward Tempe.

"Daniel!"

"It's all right, Isabel. I'll go. But I want you to think about what I said. It's time you let us know everything about Marella. Give me a call when you're ready, okay?" She held a card with her home phone number as well as the sub-station's on it in Isabel's direction.

Daniel tried to snatch it out of Tempe's fingers but Isabel moved faster. She tucked the card into the pocket of her cut-offs.

With her hand on the door, Tempe looked at Isabel hoping to see something in her expression that would promise a more successful meeting at a later date. But Isabel's attention was fully directed toward her brother.

"Oh, Danny. You promised you weren't going to drink anymore."

Daniel pushed past his sister and stumbled toward the kitchen. Tempe stepped outside.

She felt disappointment. Because she was unsuccessful, she doubted Morrison would give her another chance to question Isabel. Positive Isabel held the key to the murder, somehow Tempe had to gain the girl's confidence so that she would reveal Marella's secrets.

The sun beat down on her as she crossed the parched yard to the Bronco. There was nothing to do but go home.

* * *

Hutch was in the kitchen putting groceries away. He frowned when she entered. "In uniform already? Something going on?"

"I was called in to the Sergeant's office."

"Really? What for?" Hutch put three different kinds of lettuce into the crisper drawer of the refrigerator.

"Seems someone registered a complaint against me."

Tempe picked up an apple from a bowl of fruit on the table and took a bite.

Hutch straightened himself and gazed at her with

genuine concern. "Oh, dear. Not anything serious, I hope."

"Grossly exaggerated. Anyway, it turned out okay."

She took another bite. She didn't really want to go into detail because she hadn't told Hutch about her confrontation with Katherine Davelos the day before.

He blinked his eyes a couple of times and tilted his head. "Is that all you're going to tell me? I have the feeling there's a lot more."

Tempe inhaled deeply. "Why don't you let me help with the groceries?"

"I'm nearly through, as you can see."

"I'm starved. I'll make some lunch."

"You'll get your uniform dirty. Why don't you sit down and tell me what went on this morning while I fix something to eat. How about a mushroom and cheese omelet?"

"Sounds wonderful. I'll fix the toast." She reached for the loaf of bread. Hutch grabbed her hand. "Please, sit down. I can handle it."

She pulled out a chair and sat. "Katherine Davelos said I accosted and badgered her, and accused her of murder."

"When did you see her?" Hutch began breaking eggs into a bowl.

"Yesterday. She was at the lake near the accident."

Tempe noticed Hutch's broad shoulders sagged a bit. "Since she was there, I didn't see what it would hurt to ask her a few questions."

Not turning, Hutch asked, "Did you find out anything helpful from her?"

"Not really."

He melted butter in a frying pan. "But it was important enough to take up your time so you couldn't do what you'd promised me."

"That's not what kept me from getting to the bank on time, Hutch. I told you about the accident. I turned the investigation over to the CHP that arrived on the scene but I still had to explain everything and write and file a report."

He didn't say anything for a moment. He poured the beaten eggs into the frying pan and reached into the refrigerator for a small dish with sliced mushrooms and grated cheese. Obviously, he'd prepared for their lunch. The gesture erased the irritation she'd felt. She went to him and pressed herself against his back. "I love you, Hutch. I'm sorry I didn't get the banking done for you but I couldn't help it, really."

With the dish still in one hand, he turned around. "I love you too, Tempe." He caressed her shoulder with his other hand. "While I finish cooking, tell me the rest."

"Both the Sergeant and Morrison bawled me out for questioning Mrs. Davelos," Tempe said, and paused waiting for Hutch's comment.

Using the spatula, he poked at the eggs. "I can understand how they might be getting kind of irritated at you since they've told you over and over to stay out of the investigation."

"I don't think they're mad anymore. Morrison realizes now that there were a few things he should have been checking out." She described everything that had happened in Guthrie's office while the omelet finished cooking.

As he served the lunch, he said, "And I suppose you rushed right out to the reservation."

"Of course I did. I know Isabel holds the key to this whole investigation."

Hutch bowed his head and blessed the food, Tempe waited impatiently for him to finish so she could tell him what happened at the Redwing's.

Following the Amen, he peppered his omelet and handed the shaker to Tempe. "Did she talk to you?"

Tempe nodded.

"And you found out who the murderer is?" Hutch put forkful of eggs into his mouth.

"Well, not exactly. Isabel was coming really close to telling me something important when her brother arrived. Seems his boss was a friend of the Celsos. Because Daniel is a suspect in the murder, he was fired from his job."

"Poor kid. He certainly has his problems." Hutch took another bite.

"Unfortunately, he's trying to solve them with alcohol. He was drunk when he came in."

"Something wrong with your omelet?" Hutch

asked, pointing with his fork.

"What? I don't think so...why?"

"You haven't tasted it."

"Oh, sorry." Tempe popped some into her mouth and chewed thoughtfully. "Mmmmm, very good."

"I'd like to help that young man. It's understandable why he's so bitter but if he keeps going he'll get himself into even more trouble."

"Do you really think you could help him? He didn't sound like he wanted anything to do with a minister." She ate more of the omelet--it really was good and she realized how hungry she was.

"I'd like to at least try. Didn't you ever feel like there was something that you were supposed to do?"

"Yes, Hutch...that's exactly how I feel about finding out who murdered Marella." She reached across the table and clasped Hutch's free hand. "And if I do, that will help Daniel...if he didn't do it."

Hutch carefully placed his fork on the plate beside the uneaten half of his meal. "If you have an overpowering urge to do this, I guess I can understand. But I can't help feeling angry when you neglect us to do something you don't really have to do. Your job is bad enough. Doesn't it bother you that you are taking time away from your home and family to do this extra investigating?"

Finally he'd put into words what disturbed him. "I used to feel guilty about not spending enough time with Blair but he isn't home enough himself anymore to miss me. I am sorry you're feeling neglected. But, sweetheart, I warned you before we ever got married. Actually, you've surprised me."

"Surprised you?" Hutch tipped his head. "Surprised about what?"

"I didn't think we'd have this problem."

"Why not?"

Tempe smiled. "Because of your occupation, I suppose."

"Because I'm a minister doesn't mean I'm not human. I have all the same emotions as any other man, and sometimes I don't control them very well. I guess that's what's been happening to me lately." His eyes searched her face. His freckles stood out on his cheeks, his thick hair needed combing. He reminded her of a little boy desperate for a hug.

After pushing her chair back, she went around the table to Hutch and wiggled her way onto his lap. Putting her arms around his neck, she pressed her forehead against his. "I love you so much, and I'm so glad you're my husband." She kissed his lips lightly, again and again.

Between kisses, he breathed, "Aren't you afraid you'll mess up your uniform?"

* * *

While Tempe braided her hair, still damp from the shower she'd shared with Hutch after they made love, he asked, "When do you plan to see Isabel again?"

Startled by his question, Tempe said, "I've been

too busy to even think about that."

"May I go along next time? I'd really like another opportunity to talk with Daniel."

She folded the long braid at the back of her head and fastened it with a silver barrette. "Sure, but I don't know when that will be."

Hutch put his arms around her waist and nuzzled the back of her neck. "Maybe we can visit them this weekend. I think I'll go up to the chapel this evening after supper and get started on my sermon."

Before she could comment, Blair hollered from the kitchen, "Hey! Where is everyone!"

She giggled. "Goodness, Blair could have walked in any time."

"What's wrong with that? Don't you think he knows we make love?" Hutch asked.

"Well, sure but..."

"Sometimes you are so silly." Hutch opened the bedroom door. "We'll be right out, Blair."

Tempe heard the refrigerator door open and sounds of Blair rummaging through it. Hutch kissed her on the cheek. "You finish getting ready for work. I'll see if I can help Blair find something to eat."

By the time Tempe got out to the kitchen, Blair was gnawing on a leftover chicken leg and something was being heated up in the microwave. "Hi, Mom," Blair said. She kissed him on the forehead.

He grinned up at her. "Glad to see you and Hutch have made up."

Feeling herself blush, Tempe turned away quickly.

"Do you want anything to eat before you go?" Hutch asked.

She glanced at her watch. "No, it's getting late.

"I'll put together a snack that you can stop by and eat later."

"Thanks."

Hutch put his arms around her and kissed her goodbye. Blair watched with a pleased expression.

* * *

The first half of her shift, Tempe helped a rancher round up a half dozen head of cattle that had managed to trample down a fence and were blocking the highway. She also stopped a speeding logging truck; the logger thanked her when she handed him the ticket--something that never happened to a male deputy.

An illegal camp fire got out of hand, and Tempe joined the fire truck and volunteers who arrived to put it out. She was surprised that Blair didn't turn up.

The culprits who started the fire were no-where around; the fire quickly quenched. Hunger pangs reminded Tempe of Hutch's promised snack, and she decided to take a break.

* * *

Hutch's blue and white truck was gone, but Blair's yellow bug was still parked in the driveway. Again she wondered why he hadn't turned up at the fire. Before she got out of the Blazer, Blair exploded from the back door. "Am I glad you're here!"

"What's the matter? Are you sick? Is there something wrong with Hutch?"

Blair shook his blond head. "No, Mom, nothing like that. Isabel Redwing called."

"Do you know Isabel?"

Impatiently, Blair said, "Of course I know her, we're in the same grade at school. But listen to me, Mom, this is important."

"I'm sorry. What is it?"

"She said her brother has a gun and he said something about coming up here to see you!"

16

"Let's go in the house, Blair." Tempe entered first. "Now tell me exactly what Isabel said."

"She sounded hysterical. It was kind of hard to understand her. She screamed that her brother had a gun and he was coming up here." Blair looked worried.

"Did she say he wanted to shoot me?"

"No." Blair thought for a moment. "But why else would he be coming up here with a gun if he wasn't planning on shooting someone?"

"People carry guns around for many reasons...most of them not good. Perhaps he thinks he needs the protection."

Blair put his hand on her shoulder. "Come on, Mom, protection from you? Shouldn't you report this to your dispatcher or something? I don't want anything to happen to you."

"Nothing is going to happen. Daniel doesn't have any reason to shoot me."

"Why does he want to see you?"

"That I don't know. But I suspect I'll find out pretty soon." Tempe pulled open the refrigerator. "Where's that snack Hutch promised to fix? I'm starving."

"Mom! How can you eat when you know this guy is coming up here gunning for you?"

She brought out a plate covered with plastic wrap. "Umm, this looks yummy." Pieces of rare roast beef were artistically arranged on a plate beside asparagus spears and tomato slices.

"Mother!"

Tempe sat down to eat. "When did you get this phone call?"

Blair began pacing. "I don't know. Half-an-hour ago, maybe."

"Then I better hurry and eat, he ought to be turning up here any minute now."

"If you won't call your dispatcher, at least call Hutch and tell him what's going on."

Tempe cut a piece of meat and popped it into her mouth. "Do you know Daniel Redwing?"

"I know what he looks like, but I don't know him. He was a couple of grades ahead of me in school. He was on the wrestling team, did real good. But what does that matter? He's coming up here with a gun!" Blair put his hands on the table and leaned down near Tempe.

"Calm down, Blair. I do know Daniel and I don't

think he's planning to shoot me. Why don't you sit down?" Blair dropped into the chair opposite her, but continued to gaze at her like she'd lost her mind.

"Did you know Marella Celso too?" Tempe asked, wondering why she'd never thought about the fact Marella was a senior at Dennison High just like Blair.

"Of course. Everyone knew Marella. She was real popular."

"Why?"

Blair shrugged. "How would I know? She was great looking and had a good personality."

"It didn't matter that she was Indian?"

"Maybe to a few kids, but most thought it was cool that she was a native American."

Times had changed since Tempe went to school. "Tell me more about her."

"She was friendly to everyone. Not stuck up like some of the other pretty girls."

"Did she have a boyfriend at school?"

"Not anyone in particular. I heard she was going steady with someone who graduated already."

"Cody Endrezza," Tempe prompted.

"Yeah, that's right," Blair said.

"What do you know about him?"

"Don't remember him very well. A jock. Think he played basketball. Mostly hung around with other Native Americans. But that's kind of the way it is. The Mexicans hang around with Mexicans, the Asians with Asians, the Blacks with Blacks, Anglos with

Anglos. Mostly, anyway. Marella was kind of the exception, she was friends with everyone." Someone knocked on the back door and Blair jumped to his feet, looking anxiously at Tempe. She kept eating.

"Should I answer it?"

"Unless you want me to."

Opening the door only a couple of inches, he peeked out. Turning toward Tempe, Blair said, "It's him, Mom. What do you want me to do?"

"Invite him in." Tempe wiped her mouth on a napkin and turned in her chair.

Blair opened the door wide and stepped back barely enough to allow Daniel inside. Blair pushed the door shut, and towering over their uninvited guest. He glowered.

Daniel ignored Blair's threatening demeanor. Hair neatly slicked back into its pony tail, Daniel wore an unbuttoned short-sleeved shirt over a T-shirt, and clean but faded Levis. He appeared to have sobered up since Tempe's encounter with him earlier in the day.

"What can I do for you, Redwing?" Tempe asked.

"I want you to stay away from my sister!" Daniel growled.

"Hey! Don't talk to my mother like that," Blair said, moving within inches of the young man.

Daniel still didn't take his eyes away from Tempe.

"It's okay, Blair," Tempe said. "Why don't you go up to the fire station or something."

"I'm not about to leave you here alone with this

guy. Don't forget about the gun."

Daniel jerked his head to look at Blair, his dark brows nearly meeting over his aquiline nose.

"Who told you about a gun?"

"Isabel called. She's very upset. Do you have a gun, Daniel?"

"That's none of your business," Daniel snapped.

"Actually, it is my business." Tempe stood. "If you do have a gun why don't you give it to me right now? It would make me and my son feel much more comfortable." She held out her hand.

Redwing again glanced at Blair who had drawn himself up to his full height and swelled out his chest, and back at Tempe. "Damn," he muttered, reaching behind his back and under his shirt, bringing out a small revolver. Carefully, he placed it into Tempe's hand.

"Where'd you get this?"

"It's my Mom's. She keeps it beside her bed."

"Does she know you have it?"

"No. Are you going to give it back to me so she won't find out?"

Tempe opened it and checked the cylinder.

"It isn't loaded," he said.

"I can see that." She put it down on the table.

"It's not too smart for you to be carrying a gun. That's against the law, you know."

"What difference does it make? Everyone already thinks I killed Marella."

Blair frowned and shot a questioning glance at his

mother.

"I don't," Tempe said. "Why don't you tell me what was so important that you thought you had to come up here with a gun."

Redwing raised his hands. "Oh, what's the use! Nothing is working out for me these days."

"Why don't you tell me what's troubling you, Daniel," Tempe coaxed. She pulled out the chair she'd been sitting in. "I think it's easier to talk sitting down."

Collapsing into the chair, Redwing leaned forward as Tempe sat across from him. Blair continued standing as though ready to pounce if necessary.

Tempe had difficulty to keep from grinning at her son's protectiveness. "Now, Daniel, what's this all about."

"It's Isabel, she's been crying ever since you left. I can't stand it. I came up here to tell you to stay away from her. She didn't do anything. You're making her miserable."

"You're wrong, Daniel, I'm not making her miserable."

"Then what is?"

"She knows something about Marella, something that would help us find out who killed her. Because she promised Marella to keep whatever it is a secret, she doesn't think she should tell me. But she's torn. I think deep down Isabel realizes she should tell me. That whatever it is she knows would clear you and point out the real murderer."

Daniel's face clouded. "You really think she knows something that would prove I didn't do it?"

"Yes, I do."

"No, that can't be it. Isabel loves me. She would do anything to help me."

"That's the whole problem. No wonder she's been crying all day. She wants to help you...but she feels this tremendous loyalty for her best friend and to the promise she made to keep the secret Marella entrusted to her."

Daniel blinked his dark eyes. "If you're right...how can we get her to tell you?"

As Redwing's attitude improved, Blair backed away until he reached the refrigerator. He leaned against it, jamming his hands in the pockets of his denim pants.

"I'm not sure. But I have an idea. Why don't we go up to the chapel where my husband is working? He might have some suggestion for us. He's been wanting to talk to you anyway."

Frowning, Daniel said, "I don't know. I don't have any use for preachers."

"Hutch is an okay guy," Blair put in.

Redwing thought again. "Okay. But if he starts putting down my beliefs, I'm going to leave."

"Fair enough," Tempe stood. "I'll drive you. Blair, give Hutch a call and let him know we're on the way."

"What about the gun?" Daniel asked.

"I'll bring it out to your place tomorrow."

Though he seemed reluctant to leave it, he obviously realized any argument was futile.

It was nearly ten o'clock. The Cafe was closed. Only a few cars were parked in front of The Saloon. The fire trucks were back in place at the station with a pale light coming from the office into the open garage. The town of Bear Creek was nearly deserted. As Tempe drove on through, past the Bear Creek Inn, she noted that most of the downstairs lights were out and the parking lot was empty.

Tempe made the turn-off to the chapel. The A-frame church, built of weathered cedar, was surrounded by a thick growth of pine, aspen, silver and valley oaks. As they approached, Redwing shifted uneasily. "I'm not so sure this is a good idea...."

"Everything will be fine." Tempe led the way into the dark sanctuary, moonlight reflecting through the stained glass window at the front spattered the altar and the first row of pews with splashes of pastel hues. The door to Hutch's office stood ajar, a yellow rectangle welcoming them.

An obvious structural addendum, the small room was comfortably furnished with a worn couch and plump armchair. Hutch came around his desk, a slab set upon two-drawer file cabinets, his hand extended toward Redwing. He grinned broadly, showing his dimple.

"Daniel! I'm so glad to see you."

With obvious reluctance, Redwing allowed Hutch

to shake his hand, taking his own back quickly. He peered around nervously at the shelves overflowing with books, the modern paintings of Christ hanging on the walls. "Pastor."

"I was getting ready to come home when Blair called. I must say I was surprised. I have some coffee made, anyone want any?"

"I guess." Redwing made his way to the armchair but stood as though waiting for permission to sit.

"I'll pour." Tempe said going to the coffee maker sitting on a card table near the door. She filled two Styrofoam cups. "Daniel and I were hoping that you might have some suggestions as to how we can convince his sister she should tell me what Marella told her."

Still standing, Redwing nodded his head.

"Cream, sugar?" Tempe asked as she handed him a cup.

"Black is fine."

"Go ahead and sit down," Tempe directed as she settled herself on the end of the couch nearest Daniel.

Hutch leaned against his desk. He took off his glasses and tucked them into his shirt pocket.

Tempe once again explained how she thought Isabel held the key to the mystery, but her promise to Marella kept her from revealing whatever secrets Marella had entrusted in her. As she spoke Hutch nodded his head thoughtfully.

"I think you have the answer, Tempe. Isabel has

to be convinced that she will not be betraying Marella by telling you...but instead be giving you a means of clearing her brother."

"But how is the Deputy going to do that, Pastor?" Redwing asked. "She explained all that to my sister this morning. Isabel wouldn't tell her anything."

"I think she was coming really close when you interrupted us, Daniel," Tempe said.

"Sorry about how I acted. I was drinking. Are you going to try talking to her again?"

"I plan to see her in the morning."

"Good." Redwing looked relieved and started to get up.

"Wait," Hutch said. "Why don't we talk about your drinking. Sounds like you might be ready to do something about that."

"Here we go," Redwing said. "I knew it would be like this if I came up here. You preachers are all alike."

"I only want to help."

Redwing's deep set eyes flashed. "You don't know what I've been going through."

"Of course I don't. Would you like to tell me about it?"

"You wouldn't understand. You've got everything you want...a good job, no worries, married to the woman you love."

"You're right. I have been blessed lately, Daniel, and I'm thankful to God for those blessings. But what you don't know is my first wife died. I was very much in love with her. I still remember how painful my loss was...and the terrible loneliness. That hurt and pain never totally go away, but they do lessen with time. Why don't you tell me about your hurt and pain?"

Daniel gulped some of his coffee before setting the cup aside on the corner of the desk. "I loved Marella, but she didn't love me. When I found out Cody had asked her to marry him and she said yes, I wanted to die. But it was funny, she didn't treat me any different after that. She was still nice. I kept hoping something might happen between them, and I would be right there to take his place. I used to dream about that."

After wiping his thighs with the heels of his hands, Daniel continued. "She used to come over to the house to visit Isabel, and I felt miserable and thrilled all at the same time. I suppose I drank to keep it from hurting so much.

"Now everyone thinks I killed Marella. That's so crazy. I would never, never have done anything to hurt her. The girl I loved is dead, I'll probably go to jail for her murder. Tell me any good reason why I shouldn't drink, Pastor? What else is there for me?"

"My wife is determined to find out who killed Marella, and when she does that will clear your name. That won't bring Marella back, of course. But when I lost my first wife, I turned to God for help."

Redwing shifted uneasily. Tempe's radio squawked. It was the dispatcher summoning her to investigate a prowler.

"I've got to go. Will you bring Daniel back to the house?"

As Tempe left, she heard Hutch saying, "I don't think our beliefs are really that far apart, Daniel."

17

After knocking several times on the door to the Redwing's mobile home and receiving no answer, Tempe wished she'd taken the time to call before coming. Hutch had reported that his meeting with Daniel had gone extremely well, causing Tempe to expect the young man to prepare his sister for her visit. Obviously something had gone awry.

In order not to intimidate Isabel, Tempe had dressed casually in a sleeveless T-shirt, denim pants, and sneakers. She had Mrs. Redwing's revolver was tucked unobtrusively in a paper bag.

Neither Daniel's truck nor the orange Datsun that Tempe presumed belonged to Mrs. Redwing were in sight. Tempe stood on the rickety porch gazing down the road, hoping to see one of the vehicles heading towards her. But hoping didn't make it happen.

She returned to the Bronco, wondering what to do next. After locking the gun in the glove compartment, she decided since she was on the reservation, she'd drive around a bit and perhaps might come across Daniel or Isabel.

Tempe cruised slowly along the road that wound through the center of the reservation. After reaching the far end, she turned around and came back, this time going up the various lanes that meandered into the hills.

When she'd almost come to the exit out of reservation land, she followed a winding track ending near the river. Tempe spotted an older model, yellow Mustang with black flames painted on the hood parked under a carport attached to a flat roofed, low slung house. Katherine Davelo's car. Maybe Tempe's day wouldn't be wasted after all.

A brick walk leading to the front door dissected a fenced-in rectangle of thick grass. Purple-and-white Shasta daisies bloomed in wooden containers beneath two plate glass windows. Drapes had been closed against the hot mid-morning sun.

Tempe rang the bell and the door opened almost instantly. Linda Davelos smiled shyly at her. "Hi, Deputy Crabtree, won't you come in?"

Stepping inside the living room, it took a moment for Tempe's eyes to adjust to the darkness. When they did, she could see the room was decorated with Indian artifacts. A turquoise, red-and-white Navajo rug was prominently displayed on the floor. The tables held Southwestern pottery, Kachina dolls and Indian statuary. Paintings depicting Native American life adorned the walls.

"How are you doing, Linda?" Tempe asked. "Anxious for school to start?"

A smile brightened Linda's round face. "Yes, ma'am. I love school."

"Is your mother around? I'd like to talk to her."

The smile disappeared. "Not exactly."

"Isn't that her Mustang parked out there?"

"Yes. But she's not inside. She's down by the river collecting reeds and stuff."

"Maybe I'll just go down and see if I can find her."

Linda frowned. "I don't know if that's a good idea. She's...well, she's kind of mad at you."

"Yes, I know."

Linda shifted nervously from one bare foot to the other. "I really don't think my mother killed Marella."

"I don't think she did either. But it would help if she'd answer my questions."

"I love my mother," Linda said.

"I'm sure you do."

"I'm sorry I'm not the kind of girl she wants...and I'm never going to be."

"She'll realize that one of these days."

Linda smiled sadly. "I hope so. Being a mom isn't one of her highest priorities."

"She's truly lucky to have a daughter like you."

"Thank you."

"I think I'll take my chances and see if I can locate her."

Tempe left the house and made her way down the hill toward the river. This branch of Bear Creek was little more than a stream. Tempe spotted Katherine several yards away, wading along the edge of the water. She wore the same bikini, her black page-boy hanging around her face as she leaned over to examine plants growing on the bank. She held a small book in one hand.

Tempe decided not to call out to her. When she came up behind her, she said softly, "Mrs. Davelos."

"Who?" Katherine spun around, nearly losing her balance. When she saw it was Tempe, she frowned. "Oh, you again. Don't you ever give up?" She closed the book and tucked it under her arm, but not before Tempe saw that it had illustrations identifying different types of herbs and plants.

"I don't think you want me to give up, Mrs. Davelos. I'm trying to find out who killed Marella. Right now you are still one of the suspects. It would be in your best interest to answer my questions."

Katherine sighed. She looked different somehow, and Tempe realized it was because she wasn't wearing her false eyelashes or any make-up. She seemed younger, more vulnerable, and prettier. And because the other woman wasn't wearing shoes, Tempe was much taller.

"It's against my principles to talk to you. I didn't kill Marella...my saying so ought to be enough. But I can see you just aren't going to be happy until I've answered your foolish questions."

"They aren't so foolish, Mrs. Davelos. If you would just clear up a few things, I could put my energies into following other clues."

Lifting her pointed chin and narrowing her eyes, Katherine said, "The Sergeant told me you didn't have any part in the investigation. That you weren't supposed to be questioning anyone."

"That was right at the time. But now he's given me his permission to do some investigating on my own." That wasn't exactly true--he'd only told her she could talk to Isabel, but Katherine didn't need to know that.

"Okay, okay. What is it you want to know?"

"Where did you get the money you put into the ticket box right before the winner of the Princess contest was announced?"

Katherine carefully made her way out of the water, stepping gingerly over the rocks lining the stream bed. She came up the grassy bank toward Tempe, her head still down, the wings of the black page boy hiding her expression. "What would you say if I told you it was Linda's money?"

"That you were lying because Two John told me you didn't put any stubs into your daughter's box."

Lifting her face, Katherine shielded her eyes against the sun with her hand. "Okay. It was Marella's money."

"How did you get it?"

Again she sighed. "I found Marella's body. The

money and the stubs were on the ground beside her."

"So you picked them up."

"Yes. At first I was going to put the stubs into Linda's box, but I noticed that Marella had marked them with her initials. So I just threw them away."

"Why didn't you tell anyone Marella was dead?"

"Because, just like you, they would have blamed me for her murder. Besides, I saw you headed in that direction, figured you'd find her soon enough."

"What made you go over there, Mrs. Davelos? There weren't any Pow Wow activities beyond the fence."

Katherine glanced down quickly before continuing. She went on without making eye contact with Tempe. "I saw Daniel Redwing come around the corner of the exhibition building. He was acting funny. Looking all around and then he started running. After he came through the gate he ducked back behind the restrooms. I just wanted to see what he'd been up to."

Tempe didn't say anything. She'd believed Katherine up until she started talking about Daniel. It sounded like she was trying to avert suspicion from herself.

"Why didn't you tell the detectives about this?"

Katherine shrugged. "I don't know."

"It's hard for me to accept the fact that you saw Redwing coming from the murder scene just before you found the body, and never mentioned that fact to anyone until now."

"I knew it wouldn't help to explain anything to you." Katherine stomped up the hill toward the house.

The sound of a rifle being fired startled Tempe and she realized someone was shooting at them. Acting instinctively, Tempe threw herself at Katherine, knocking her down.

"What the heck do you think you're doing?" Katherine said, trying to get up.

Another shot was fired. Tempe pushed Katherine's head down and she heard the bullet whiz overhead. Obviously, Katherine did too because she began shaking.

"What's going on? Who's shooting?"

"I don't know, I can't see anyone." Tempe lifted herself just enough to peer in the direction the shots came from. A black figure silhouetted against the bright sky disappeared over the crest of the hillside behind Katherine's house. In the few seconds that Tempe saw the person, her impression was whoever it was wore a hat with a brim and was limping slightly.

"It's okay, we can get up now." Tempe stood, dusting off her trousers and hands.

Katherine hesitated before rising. "My God, that scared me to death. Why would someone shoot at us?" She seemed oblivious to the dirt on her face and body.

"I have no idea. Who lives on the other side of the hill?"

"That crazy old man Whitcomb."

"Thanks for cooperating with me," Tempe said, hurrying away. She wanted to report the shooting, and then drive up to Whitcomb's place. If she found him with a rifle, she'd arrest him.

"Hey! What about me? What if the person starts shooting again?" Katherine called after her.

"You don't have to worry, whoever it was is gone." Tempe kept running toward the Bronco.

"How can you be sure?" Katherine gasped as she tried to catch up to Tempe, her progress impeded by her bare feet.

"I saw him take off. I'm going after him now."

"It was that crazy old man, wasn't it?"

"I don't know, I couldn't see well enough to identify the person." But what Tempe had seen made her suspect Whitcomb. She reached the Bronco and snatched open the door.

Tempe used her radio to report the shooting.

When Tempe started to drive off, Katherine hollered after her, "Are you coming back? Are you going to let me know who it was?"

"Not today," Tempe said out the window just before heading out to the main road. In the rear view mirror, she could see Katherine with one hand on her hip, the plant book still tucked under her arm.

Driving up the hill toward Whitcombs', Tempe glanced from one side of the lane to the other, in search of the old rancher--or anyone else. But all she spotted was a ground squirrel that darted across her path, several head of cattle near the black pond, and a pair of ducks circling overhead.

Whitcomb's truck was parked near the front of the castle house. As Tempe passed it on her way to the door, she rested her hand on the hood. The metal was only warm from the sun.

Tempe lifted her fist to knock, but the door opened before her knuckles made contact with the wood.

With her dried apple face knotted into a frown, Alice said, "Deputy Crabtree. What can I do for you?"

Tempe peered past Alice down the long hallway leading to the kitchen. "Is your brother around?"

"He's outside working. He is a rancher you know. He does have work to do." Alice blocked the doorway. Her friendly attitude toward Tempe on her prior visit had vanished.

Before Tempe could comment, Grant's gravely voice came from the back of the house. "Alice! Alice! Where have you gotten yourself?"

"I'm here, Grant. We've got company," she warned.

But Whitcomb was already on his way toward them. "Couldn't find the s.o.b.s but..." He stopped when he finally realized who his sister was talking to.

A rifle was propped over his arms, held by his gnarled hands. His straw hat perched above his over-sized ears. "What the Sam Hill are you doing here again? Ain't you got nothing better to do than pester us law abiding citizens?" He limped to his sister's side.

"I'm here to question you about a shooting that just occurred near the edge of your ranch. Have you fired that rifle recently, Mr. Whitcomb?"

A nerve twitched near his nose and he snarled, "I got a right to fire my gun to protect my property!"

"You didn't answer my question. Did you fire that gun in the last half hour?"

"I can't see where it's any of your business. Don't look like you're on duty, Deputy." He looked her up and down contemptuously.

"Mr. Whitcomb, I'm losing my patience."

"Okay, okay. Them damn Indians been after my cattle again. I fired a couple of warning shots, that's all. I wasn't trying to hit anyone."

"Where were you when you fired those warning shots?" Tempe asked.

Alice's expression was undergoing a metamorphosis from irritation to apprehension.

Whitcomb lifted his hat and smoothed back his sparse sandy hair. "I dunno, for sure. I was too busy chasing after them daggone hooligans."

"When you say chased...what do you mean exactly? Were you running after them?"

Dropping his hat back onto his head, Whitcomb glared at her. "I ain't no spring chicken anymore, woman. Of course, I wasn't running. I was on horseback."

"You fired the rifle while riding a horse?" Tempe remembered the figure that she'd seen running with a distinct limp over the crest of the hill.

"You're trying my patience, Deputy. I don't know how much plainer I can say it. Yes, I was riding after them varmints on my horse. When I saw I wasn't going to catch up, I fired over their heads. Give 'em something to think about."

Though the silhouette of the person who'd shot at her and Katherine resembled Mr. Whitcomb, he or she had been too far away for Tempe to be sure who it was. "I think it would be a good idea for you to put your rifle away. When you spot someone trespassing on your land, why don't you call the sub-station? Let a deputy handle the problem."

Whitcomb laughed humorlessly. "Are you kidding? By the time one of you bozos got out here, those savages could rustle my whole herd! Besides, I got reason to believe the Sheriff's Department is in cahoots with the Indians."

Tempe had heard Whitcomb spout his conspiracy theory before. "The only side we're on is the side of the law," she said, knowing it wouldn't make any difference to the old rancher.

"I'm going to leave now, Mr. Whitcomb. But I want you to be careful with that rifle. You don't want to hurt anyone accidentally."

"If I hurt anyone, it ain't gonna be no accident!"

"Grant." Alice grasped her brother's arm. "Maybe

you ought to..."

"Don't be telling me what to do, woman." He wrenched his arm out of his sister's grasp. "Hey, deputy, what brought you back up here anyway? Them daggone savages been talking about me?"

"No, Mr. Whitcomb, no one has even mentioned you lately. But someone who looked a lot like you just took some potshots at Katherine Davelos and me." Without waiting for a comment, Tempe started toward her car.

She heard Alice say, "Oh, Grant, surely you didn't...."

Whitcomb interrupted with, "Hush your mouth!" followed by the sound of the heavy door being slammed shut.

18

Tempe glanced at her watch. Too late to go back to the reservation to see if Isabel had returned. As she climbed into the Bronco, her radio crackled to life.

The call was for her. After Tempe identified herself, the dispatcher said, "Sergeant Guthrie's been trying to contact you by land line. He wants you to report into the station immediately."

Before Tempe could ask any questions the dispatcher had signed off. What now? There hadn't been time for Mr. Whitcomb to make a complaint about her. Looking down at her dirt-stained T-shirt and denims, she knew she wasn't dressed for a command appearance at the sub-station, but there wasn't anything she could do about it.

* * *

Stepping into Sergeant Guthrie's office, Tempe wasn't surprised to see both Detectives Morrison and Richards already settled into the two upholstered chairs. Without saying anything, she seated herself on the folding chair.

"Been gardening, Crabtree?" Richards asked, squinting at her disheveled appearance.

"What is this about someone shooting at you and Katherine Davelos?" Guthrie snapped.

Morrison poked his ugly face around his partner. "What were you doing there anyway? Didn't we tell you to leave that woman alone?"

Tempe patiently waited until they were through with their ranting and raving.

When Guthrie snarled, "Well?" she began.

"I went to see Isabel Redwing this morning but she wasn't there."

"I thought you were going to see her yesterday," Morrison said.

Richards turned to his partner. "You gave her permission to question Daniel Redwing's sister?"

Morrison pulled away. "It seemed like a good idea at the time. Crabtree thinks the girl has the key to the murder."

Without showing any emotion on his long, squinty face, Richards once again faced Tempe. "And so what amazing information did you learn?"

"Isabel was just about to open up to me when Daniel came in and interrupted us. But after talking to her, I'm even more positive than I was before that she is the solution to this whole puzzle."

"The solution is Daniel Redwing. It's just a matter of gathering enough evidence against him,"

Richards said.

"No, Detective, I don't think so. Daniel has lots of problems, but killing Marella isn't one of them."

"What makes you so sure of that?"

"Nothing concrete but...."

Morrison snorted rudely. "No shit!"

Sergeant Guthrie leaned on his desk. "You haven't explained what you were doing at the Davelos' residence this morning...or who was shooting at you."

"Daniel Redwing came to visit me last night," she began.

"What'd he do that for?" Richards asked.

The Sergeant waved his hand. "Whoa! Don't go zooming off on another track, Crabtree. You're driving me nuts, here."

"It'll be simpler if I just tell it the way things happened," Tempe said. "Daniel wasn't very happy when he arrived at my place." She decided not to mention anything about the gun.

"How come?" Richards asked. "You been harassing him too?"

Guthrie exploded. "Hey! Let Crabtree finish, okay?"

Tempe explained how Daniel was upset because his sister had been crying since Tempe had left their home. Daniel calmed down after Tempe related to him her conviction that Isabel knew something about Marella she hadn't told anyone. Whatever the secret, it was making Isabel miserable.

"He even agreed that I should return to their house and talk to Isabel. After I went back to work, Daniel spent time with Hutch. Though I don't know what their conversation was about, Hutch said it went well. Because Daniel left in good spirits, I was anxious to meet with his sister again."

Detective Richards opened his mouth, appearing as though to ask a question but the sergeant glowered at him. Richards crossed his arms and settled back against the chair.

Tempe continued. "Unfortunately, no one was at the Redwing's when I got there. I drove around the reservation looking for them, with no luck. But I spotted Mrs. Davelos car, and decided that rather than waste the trip out there, I'd see if she might be a bit more receptive on her home ground."

"Sure don't know how to obey orders." Morrison mumbled, shutting up when the sergeant glared at him too.

"I found Mrs. Davelos down by the river. And I'm glad I talked to her. She told me what happened to Marella's ticket stubs and money."

"Just tell us about the shots, Crabtree," the Sergeant urged.

"Someone started shooting at us. We hit the dirt. I spotted someone running over the top of the hill."

"Did you get a good look at him? Who was it?"

"The sun was in my eyes, and all I could see was the silhouette. But whoever it was limped...I got the impression it might have been Grant Whitcomb."

"Why would that old codger take pot shots at you?" Richards asked.

She shrugged. "I don't have any idea. I went to see Whitcomb. He was carrying a rifle but said he'd been chasing Indians off his property."

"Do you think he was telling the truth?" the sergeant asked.

"I don't know. If it was Whitcomb who shot at us...I wonder who the target was, me...or Mrs. Davelos? And if it wasn't Whitcomb doing the shooting, it was someone who wanted us to think it was the old man."

"Why, Crabtree? Why would Whitcomb or anyone else want to shoot either one of you?" Morrison asked.

"Unless she's coming closer to the truth about this case than she realizes," Richards said. His pinched face relaxed. "Maybe you better tell us about those raffle tickets after all."

Tempe explained how Katherine had finally admitted to finding the body and taking the money and the stubs with the intention of putting the stubs into her daughter's box. "But she discovered Marella had put her initials on all of them so she just threw them away."

"That woman lied to us about lots of things," Morrison grumbled.

"I hate to admit it, but you seem to have a way of weaseling information out of these people. Must have something to do with your sex or the fact that you're part Indian," Richards said.

Tempe didn't much like his conclusions but decided it was in her best interest not to protest. Forcing a smile, she said, "Thank you. But I'm not so sure that she isn't lying to me too."

"About what?"

"Doesn't it seem strange that she wouldn't tell anyone about finding Marella's body? Maybe she's the one who killed her to make sure her daughter would become Princess."

"But it didn't work out that way," Morrison reminded her.

"No, it didn't...but she didn't know that. Supposedly, she saw Redwing running from the area where she found Marella's body. I'm not sure that's true either. She might have made it up to direct suspicion away from herself."

"I still think Redwing did it," Morrison muttered.

"I'd cast my vote for him too," Richards said. "But Crabtree has brought up some interesting points."

"There's more to all of this. And I know Isabel holds the answer."

Richards crossed his legs and smoothed the wrinkles out of his suit jacket before speaking. "My intentions were to warn you again to keep your nose out of this case, with some sort of dire threats from the Sergeant if you ignored the warning. But under the circumstances, Crabtree, I think it is in our best interest for you to continue pursuing this angle with Isabel Redwing."

Morrison and Sergeant Guthrie both looked surprised. Tempe felt grateful. "Does this mean I can go ahead and ask whatever questions I want of anyone?"

"I didn't say that!" Richards' face again squeezed into an encompassing squint.

"Hey, why not?" Morrison said, standing. "We haven't been getting anywhere. If she can make some headway with these folks, why not let her?"

"Now, wait a minute," Guthrie said, pushing himself up with his meaty palms on the top of his desk. "Crabtree is my deputy...I'm the one who gives out her assignments."

"Well, what about it, Sergeant? Can she give us a hand here?" Morrison asked.

"I can't spare her from Bear Creek. I haven't got any available men to replace her."

"What if I just do it in my spare time?" Tempe asked. Hutch wouldn't be very happy about that, but she knew she would have continued with her investigation without sanction from the detectives anyway.

"So long as it doesn't interfere with your resident deputy duties in Bear Creek," the sergeant said with obvious reluctance.

Morrison clapped the sergeant on the shoulder. "Great!"

"When do you think you'll be able to talk to Isabel again?" Richards asked.

"Probably not until tomorrow. It's pretty late now. By the time I get home and cleaned up it'll be time for me to go on duty."

Richards nodded. "Soon as you find out anything, give me a call, understand?"

"Yes, sir."

Tempe was almost out of the office when Sergeant Guthrie called after her. "Crabtree...you be careful."

Hutch was mowing the front lawn when she pulled into the driveway. She climbed out of the Bronco and he started toward her, a mixture of worry and irritation in his expression. "Where have you been? It's getting so late, I was afraid something had happened to you. How come you're so dirty?"

"It's a long story and I have to get ready for work."

"I was about to quit anyway." Hutch wiped his sweaty brow with his arm. "It's too hot for this kind of work. Have you had anything to eat?" He came to her and kissed her cheek.

"No, and I don't have time right now."

Once they were inside the house, Hutch opened the refrigerator and pulled out a pitcher. "At least have a glass of iced tea."

"That sounds wonderful. Any messages?"

"Pete Roundtree wants you to give him a call as soon as possible."

"I'd better do that now." She dialed the phone while her husband poured the tea.

When she reached the fire captain, he greeted her

enthusiastically. "Couldn't have called at a better time. Have that kid of yours off doing errands for me."

"Do you want to talk to me about Blair?" Tempe asked, wondering if something was wrong.

"There's no need to sound so worried, Tempe," Pete said. "Just wanted to know if you were going to be free Monday evening."

"Sure...I guess so. That's one of my nights off. I'll have to ask Hutch, of course."

"Oh, I already checked with him. He's okay for that night."

Tempe couldn't imagine why Pete would want to know if she and Hutch were free. "What's this all about, Pete?"

The fire captain chuckled. "We're giving Blair a surprise birthday party. Works out perfect, his birthday being on our regular meeting night. It'll be a cinch to pull this off. Thought you and your husband might like to join us."

Blair's eighteenth birthday! Tempe had forgotten completely.

"I'm gonna be mighty glad to finally be able to start paying the kid. He's my most faithful volunteer. 'Course school starts the same day, and he's talking about taking fire science courses at night at the community college. Probably won't have a heck of a lot of time for the our little fire department."

Pete's words barely registered with Tempe as waves of guilt washed over her.

"So, do you think you can make it?" he asked.

"Oh, yes. Of course."

Pete told her the arrangements for the party before hanging up. Dazed, she replaced her own receiver.

"Hutch, why didn't you tell me about Blair's party?"

"I just heard about it myself a little while ago."

"I feel terrible. I forgot all about his birthday."

Hutch handed her the glass of tea. "You've been too busy thinking about Marella's murder."

"That's no excuse."

Hutch just looked at her.

"It isn't going to get any better."

"What do you mean?"

"The detectives gave me the go-ahead to work on the murder investigation."

His gray eyes peered at her intently. "That pleases you, I'm sure."

Tempe smiled tentatively, but he didn't return the smile. "Yes, it does. But there's a catch."

"Isn't there always?"

"I have to do it on my own time."

He shook his head but didn't say anything.

Feeling like a lousy mother and wife, Tempe shrugged. "It's really late. I have to get ready for work."

"I think we need to talk, Tempe," Hutch said.

"Probably, but I just don't have time now."

His voice revealed the frustration he was feeling. "When will you have time?"

19

Tempe was glad Hutch was sound asleep when she crept in beside him. The temperature hadn't fallen many degrees after the sun went down. Whether or not it was the heat, or just people acting crazy because it was the last weekend of summer, she had an abundance of calls that ranged from domestic violence to neighbors fighting.

While she worked, she kept thinking about forgetting Blair's birthday. What kind of a mother forgot her only child's birthday? Hutch's criticism of her was valid, she'd allowed Marella's murder to become an obsession. He had every right to be irritated.

Despite everything, she could hardly wait for morning to arrive so she could drive out to the reservation to visit Isabel. Tempe felt Isabel's revelations would make it easier to figure out who had killed Marella and for what reason. Once the case was solved, Tempe could work on being the wife Hutch expected and the mother Blair deserved.

The sounds and tantalizing smells of breakfast awakened Tempe. It was after nine. If she wanted to see Isabel today, she had to hurry.

When she walked into the kitchen wearing her uniform, Hutch's expression revealed his disappointment. "Thought you might sleep in this morning."

"How could I with such yummy smells coming from the kitchen." She snagged a piece of bacon from a plate on the stove.

Hutch poured her a cup of coffee. "Obviously you're planning to work this morning."

"I have to talk to Isabel Redwing." She sipped the coffee.

"Kind of thought you might want to go shopping for a present for Blair." Hutch leaned against the sink.

Tempe sighed. "I would love to do that, but I just can't. The sooner I talk to Isabel the faster this whole mess will be cleared up."

"That's what you think, anyway." Hutch brought a baking pan from the oven. "Coffee cake. I made it this morning. It was a real hit with Blair."

"Smells heavenly. Let me call Isabel first." Tempe tried to ignore her husband's wounded expression as she looked up the Redwing's number and dialed it.

Sounding noncommittal, Isabel agreed to Tempe's visit. After hanging up, Tempe said, "She'll see me in an hour. I've got time to enjoy your baking and your company."

Hutch sat across the table from her, watching while

she ate. "Have you even thought about a present for Blair?"

Tempe shook her head. "No, Hutch. And I already feel guilty about forgetting his birthday. But there's nothing I can do about it now."

Running his fingers through his hair, Hutch said, "No, of course there isn't. Have you got any idea what he might like? I could shop for you."

"If you wouldn't mind, I'd really appreciate it. I'd probably just buy him clothes for school and give him some money. Since he's been a teenager, unless he's given me a specific request, I haven't had much success coming up with clever gifts." She finished the coffee cake and washed it down with the last of her coffee.

"I better go."

"I wish you success," Hutch said.

"Thanks." She leaned over, circled his neck with her arms and kissed him.

Rubbing her back, he said, "I'll be glad when this is all over and you have time for us again."

"Me too, Hutch...really."

"If you see Daniel, tell him I have some suggestions for him."

Hutch's comment made Tempe realize she'd never heard the details of her husband's discussion with Daniel--and there wasn't time to go into it now. "I will."

* * *

It was so hot that by the time Tempe left the air conditioned interior of the Bronco and made her away across the yard to the rickety porch of the Redwings' mobile home, her uniform was sticking to her back. The door opened before she lifted her hand to knock.

Isabel quickly ushered her inside. "No one's home but me."

Tempe had already guessed that since neither Daniel's battered truck nor Mrs. Redwing's Datsun were parked outside. "My husband wanted me to give your brother a message, perhaps you can do that for me."

Shrugging, Isabel said. "If I see him. He didn't come home last night. Please, sit down."

The part of the house Tempe could see was as neat as before; she sat on one end of the worn couch, Isabel the other. Though the swamp cooler hummed, the damp air only served to make Tempe feel stickier. "My husband wants to talk to Daniel."

Isabel looked eager. "Does he know about a job for him? If Daniel could find another job I know it would make all the difference. But who's going to hire him when everyone thinks he killed Marella?"

"That's what I want to talk to you about, Isabel. If you can help me, maybe together, we can prove your brother didn't have anything to do with Marella's murder."

Tucking one leg under the other, Isabel leaned toward Tempe. "You really don't think he did it, do you?"

"No, Isabel, I don't, even though Katherine Davelos told me she saw your brother coming from behind the exhibition building. Supposedly, that's why she went back there and found Marella's body."

Isabel's complexion darkened. "She's lying!"

"Why would she make up something like that?"

"I don't know except she never liked Danny."

"She could be covering for someone else, I suppose...or maybe she killed Marella and is just trying to make it look like Daniel did it. But you are going to have to open up to me, tell me everything you know about Marella. It's the only way we can find out who did kill her."

Isabel closed her eyes for a moment. When she opened them again, she looked sad. "I've been thinking about this so much. It's just about made me crazy. Marella was my best friend in the whole world. We told each other everything. Stuff we'd never tell another living soul." Isabel paused and fiddled with her fingers.

Tempe waited.

"If I tell you her secrets, I'll be betraying her. But if I don't tell you, her killer might never be found. And maybe my brother will end up going to jail."

"Nothing can hurt Marella anymore," Tempe said.

"I know. I've been thinking about everything you said the last time you were here. Maybe you're right. The only way I can help Marella is to tell you what I know. I don't see how it will help you find out who killed her but it's all I can do."

"I'm so glad you feel that way." Tempe reached out and patted the girl's arm. "Who was the father of the baby Marella was expecting?"

"I don't know why that's so hard to figure out. It was Cody's, of course."

Though Tempe had expected this answer, it brought up more questions. "If the baby was Cody's, why did Marella break up with him?"

Isabel pushed her hair behind her ears and sat up straighter. "Cody isn't the nice guy everyone thinks he is. Danny's been telling me that ever since Marella started going with him. I thought Danny was just saying that because he liked Marella too. But Marella found out for herself."

"What happened, Isabel?"

The girl stood. "Do you want something to drink?"

Tempe shook her head.

"Well, I do." She went into the kitchen and rummaged around in the refrigerator, returning to the living room carrying a soda.

Tipping the can, Isabel took a long drink before she spoke. "Marella and Cody only did it once. She didn't want to. She came to my house after it happened. She was so upset."

"Is that why she broke up with him? Because he forced her to have sex with him?"

"No. He apologized, promised he'd never do that

again. That he'd wait until they got married. Everything was okay for awhile. Until Marella told him she was pregnant."

"What happened?"

The girl was still having trouble disclosing Marella's confidences as evidenced by her actions. She paced in front of Tempe, finished drinking her coke and took the empty can into the kitchen before she spoke again.

Isabel leaned against the wall that divided the two small rooms. "Marella thought he'd be happy about the news. He was always after her to get married, to set a date. But when she told him, he got mad. First he told her to get an abortion. Marella would never do that.

But that wasn't the worst."

Again Isabel paused. Taking a deep breath she plunged ahead. "He accused her of being with someone else. He didn't think the baby was his because they'd only done it one time."

"Oh, dear. The poor girl."

"That's when Marella saw Cody for what he really is. She told him she didn't want to marry him. At first he thought she meant just not any time soon, and he was still talking about abortion. Marella just came out and informed him she didn't want to date him or see him anymore."

"I know he wouldn't accept that. I heard him arguing with her at the Pow Wow," Tempe interjected.

"It was like he just couldn't believe she wouldn't change her mind. He was after her all the time. Because her folks like him so much, he kept coming to her house."

"Surely she planned to tell them what was going on. She couldn't keep being pregnant a secret for very long."

Isabel collapsed on the couch. It was as though revealing Marella's intimate confidences had dissolved all her energy. "She planned to tell her folks after the Pow Wow. She didn't want to spoil it for them."

"I think Jake and Violet could have handled the news."

Tears welled in Isabel's eyes. "I begged her to tell them. If they had only known what Cody had put her through they never would have made her spend so much time with him. She agonized over it. They liked Cody so much, she knew it would be a blow to them."

"But I'm sure they would have believed her."

"Yes, I think so too. And so did she, really. But they were so excited about the Pow Wow, she just didn't want to do anything until after it was over."

"And she was killed before she had the chance."

Isabel sniffed and one tear slid down beside her nose. "Does any of that help you?"

"Maybe. Isabel, do you know where Cody lives? I'd like to ask him a few questions."

Cringing, Isabel said, "Oh, please, Deputy Crabtree, don't tell him I told you about him."

Tempe stood. "Don't worry, I won't let him know where I found out."

After she was driving away, Tempe remembered she still had Mrs. Redwing's gun in her glove compartment. It wouldn't hurt for her to hang on to it for a while longer.

Though her instinct was to believe everything Isabel had told her, there was always the possibility she was lying to protect her brother. And if by some chance, Tempe had misjudged both of them, it would be better if the gun was out of Daniel's reach.

Fortunately, Cody lived on the reservation too--not far from the Redwings. The Endrezza home was one of the larger and nicer homes around. Built of redwood, the house with its wrap-around deck sprawled across the large lot. Bear Creek ran below the house, a magnificent view of the hills and the Sierra behind it. In contrast to the many yards littered with abandoned cars, Tempe could see the back ends of a nearly-new Lincoln and a late model Honda Accord parked side-by-side in the open garage. A Toyota truck was parked nearby. The Endrezzas seemed to be doing all right for themselves.

Tempe hoped the vehicles meant Cody was home. As she climbed out of the Bronco, the object of her visit came around the side of the house. He wore jeans and cowboy boots. His chest was bare. Sweat glistened on his copper skin. The muscles of his torso and arms were well defined though not bulky.

He frowned when he recognized her. "What's the problem, Deputy?"

"No problem, Cody. I just wanted to ask you a few questions." Tempe walked toward him. "Is there somewhere we can get out of the sun?"

It was obvious Cody didn't want to take her inside. "Follow me." He led her around to the back of the house to a covered deck filled with patio furniture.

Though the area was shaded, it was still oppressively hot. He pointed to a chair and Tempe sat down.

Cody stood with his arms crossed, his legs apart, staring at her.

"Did you know Marella Celso was pregnant?" Tempe asked.

Cody blinked once, his expression unchanging. "Yes, she told me."

"Was it your baby, Cody?" Tempe asked.

"Maybe. I don't know for sure."

"Did you intend to marry Marella?"

Cody uncrossed his arms and pulled up a chair opposite Tempe and sat down. "Of course."

"Just exactly what was your relationship with Marella?" Tempe watched Cody carefully.

His black brows knitted together. "I just told you we were planning to get married."

"That isn't exactly true, is it, Cody? You still wanted to marry her, but she had changed her mind. Isn't that how it was?"

He shifted in the chair. "Who told you that?"

"I overheard you and Marella arguing at the Pow Wow."

"That wasn't anything...just a misunderstanding. You know how it is sometimes with lovers."

"It sounded to me like she was telling you she didn't want to see you again."

"I'm saying it wasn't anything important. She would have come around." He sounded sincere.

She decided to try something different. "Where were you around the time Marella was killed?"

He shrugged. "How would I know? I don't know when she was killed. I suppose I was around the arena somewhere."

Tempe hadn't seen him around the arena before she went looking for Marella or later when Isabel was crowned Princess. "Did you know there was an eagle feather found near Marella's body?"

"What's that supposed to mean?" Cody snapped.

"I watched you dancing. You lost one of the feathers from your outfit at that time."

"So?"

"I just wondered if you might have lost it again...or maybe another one."

Leaning forward, Cody said, "Are you accusing me of killing Marella? Because if you are, you're wrong! I cared a lot for Marella and I wanted to marry her. You can ask anyone...they'll tell you."

"How did you find out that Marella was dead?"

20

Cody blinked before answering Tempe's question. "Uh...I don't know. Someone told me. Everyone was talking about it."

"It just appears strange that I couldn't find you. Seems like you would have been around, offering your condolences to Marella's parents."

"Where are you going with this? I don't much like it. If you've got something to say to me, spit it out...otherwise, I've got other things to do." He put his fists on his hips and glared at her.

Tempe started for the steps leading down from the deck. "I'll probably want to see you again, Cody."

He shook his head. "As far as I'm concerned, there's no need."

A male voice boomed from inside the house, "Cody! What's going on out there?"

"Nothing, Dad." Cody headed toward the back door. He turned back once and looked at Tempe, his dark eyes shaded making it impossible for her to read his expression.

Though she hadn't gotten any concrete information from Cody, his inability--or his reluctance--to answer her questions was intriguing. Though he professed love for Marella, he hadn't displayed much grief over his loss. Perhaps he was just one of those men who doesn't show his emotions.

Tempe climbed in the Bronco. As she backed up she spotted a curtain pulled aside at a front window and a face looking out. One of Cody's parents, no doubt.

As she drove on the winding road leading away from the reservation, questions bombarded her.

Where was Cody when Marella's body was discovered? He hadn't been seen just before or afterwards. That was strange. And it seemed even stranger that he didn't have a ready answer as to why he wasn't anywhere around.

His evasiveness suggested guilt. But what she interpreted as evasiveness might just have been a nervous response to the fact she was a deputy. That happened to many people while being questioned.

* * *

The heat was keeping folks at home; few cars passed going either way. The brown hillsides were parched by the long summer without rain, the tall grass on the sides of the road yellow and scorched.

Though Cody certainly seemed a likely suspect, she really didn't have any more substantial evidence against him than she did any of the others.

Heat shimmered up from the asphalt in front of the Bronco; the curving road ahead quivered.

Katherine Davelos had been in the right place at the right time. If she hadn't seen Daniel coming from the other side of the exhibit hall, why did she go back there? Why didn't she report the murder? Unless, of course, she was the murderer. And she had wanted Marella out of the Princess competition. Could she really have wanted it that much?

Driving past Whitcomb's mailbox reminded Tempe of the old rancher. The murder weapon belonged to him. He'd been at the scene of the murder, and he had a motive--to hurt Jake Celso. It certainly looked like Whitcomb was the one shooting at her and Katherine the day before. If Tempe had been the target, wasn't that even more proof that he was the killer since she was the only one investigating him as a possible suspect?

Driving automatically toward the highway, Tempe continued speculating.

Though she didn't think he was the murderer, she couldn't cross Daniel Redwing off her list of suspects. He didn't have an alibi either. Obsessed by his unrequited love for Marella, his motive for killing her might have been to keep anyone else from having her.

Tempe really hadn't learned anything concrete to pass on to the detectives. Disappointed, she turned the Bronco onto the highway towards Bear Creek and her thoughts to her family.

She had almost four hours before her shift began. Perhaps the three of them could have a nice lunch together. She could ask them what they'd been doing, and share a bit of her investigation. If they could just spend a little time together, maybe Hutch wouldn't be so unhappy with her.

Neither Hutch nor Blair were at home when she arrived. Feeling frustrated she went inside. Hutch must still be shopping for Blair's birthday gift, and her son was probably at the fire station. He spent far more time there than he did at home. But hanging around the fire station was certainly better than what some other teenagers managed to get into.

The phone rang. It was Hutch.

"I'm surprised to catch you. How did the investigation go?"

"Not as well as I wanted. Where are you? I hoped we could have a nice lunch together."

"I'm on my way home. I'll pick up something. Is Blair around?"

"No."

"I better bring home enough food for him anyway, just in case he turns up. I'm afraid I'm not any more inventive than you. I just got him a bunch of clothes. With school starting, he'll need new stuff. Figured what he didn't like he can exchange."

"Thank you, Hutch. Now he won't have to know I forgot about his birthday."

* * *

Hutch arrived with a bag full of food and a pile of wrapped gifts. Blair breezed in just as Tempe came out of the bedroom from tucking the presents away in the closet.

"We're having Chinese! Great! I'm starving!" Blair dropped into his chair.

Hutch put a plate in front of him. "Help yourself."

As Tempe came close to her son she caught a whiff of smoke. "Been fighting fires again?"

"Yep. Another grass fire. That time of the year." He dipped a mound of rice out of one of the containers and onto his plate. "Came home 'cause I was hungry."

"I hope you wanted to see us too," Tempe said, reaching for the crispy noodles.

"'Course I'm glad to see you. Surprised you're here, though. Hutch told me you went out to the reservation. Find out anything interesting?" Blair didn't look up as he scooped a generous portion of chicken chop suey onto the rice.

"Not as much as I hoped for," Tempe admitted. She and Hutch divided what Blair left onto their plates.

"Was it even worth your while to go out there?" Hutch asked.

Tempe glanced up to see if he meant his comment as a criticism, but he only seemed intent upon scraping the last of the Moo Goo Gai Pan out of the container.

"Oh, yes. Isabel opened up to me. I think it made her feel better and I found out what was wrong between Marella and Cody." Tempe began eating.

Blair stopped attacking the food long enough to ask, "Aren't you going to tell us what it was?"

"I can't. I haven't even talked to the Detectives yet."

"Man! We have to get along without you while you do all this gallivanting and you aren't even going to let us in on what you found out?" Blair grinned at her, so she knew he was only kidding.

Unnecessarily, Hutch added, "It wouldn't be any more right for your mother to reveal what other people have confided in her then it would be for me to do that."

Actually, it wasn't quite the same. She'd been gathering information while on duty. Anyone she spoke to knew she would be passing everything she found out along to her superiors. It wouldn't be long before most of what she'd learned today would be a matter of public record. But she didn't want the information to get out before she told the detectives. The best way to make sure that didn't happen, was not to reveal anything.

But she didn't think it would hurt to tell them just a little more. "I talked to Cody too."

"And was he as cooperative as Isabel?" Hutch asked, interest apparent in his expression.

"Exactly the opposite. He wasn't at all happy to

see me."

"H'mmm. That's surprising, isn't it?"

"Not really, considering what Isabel told me. And that's not all." Tempe knew she ought to stop, but she couldn't help herself. "Cody didn't tell me the truth."

"What do you think that means?" Hutch asked, putting his fork down and looking intently at Tempe. Blair kept shoveling in the food.

"I'm not sure, exactly," Tempe said. "But then it's not up to me to solve the case. I'll just pass everything I learned on to the detectives and let them figure out what it all means."

"Sure you will, Mom." Blair laughed. "Anyone mind if I eat the rest of the noodles?"

Tempe tried to concentrate on her food. As soon as she was through she'd try to call the detectives and pass along what she'd learned. Maybe then she could forget about the case and focus her attention on Hutch for the remaining time left before she had to go to work. "Picking up this Chinese food was a great idea, sweetheart."

"I'll say!" Blair said. "What's the occasion, anyhow?"

"Nothing special. I just had to go downtown for something and thought it would be a nice change," Hutch said.

"Kind of unusual for you to go to town on a Saturday, Isn't it? Thought you always wrote you sermon on Saturday."

Tempe started laughing. Blair sounded just like her.

"I haven't got a chance around here," Hutch said, good-naturedly. "You needn't worry. I got a head start on my sermon yesterday, and I'll have plenty of time to finish it after your mother goes to work this afternoon."

"Hey, I didn't mean to be nosy or anything. I just know that you usually reserve your Saturdays."

"And you're quite right, Blair. Last weekend I tried something different so I could go to the Pow Wow, and it worked so well just thought I'd deviate a bit from my usual schedule again."

Blair stood and stretched. "I'm going to take a shower and watch some TV, if that's okay. I'm bushed."

"Of course," Tempe said, knowing quite well if his beeper went off he'd make an instant recovery and dash off to whatever emergency summoned the volunteers.

After Blair disappeared down the hall, Tempe and Hutch made small talk while they finished eating. While her husband straightened the kitchen, Tempe went into the bedroom to make her phone calls. She didn't have any luck locating either one of the detectives, leaving messages at their office at sheriff's headquarters in Visalia, the Dennison substation, and on their answering machines at their residences. With a twinge of annoyance she thought both men must be enjoying their weekend off.

Hutch was drying his hands on a dish towel when she came back into the kitchen. "I can tell by your face you didn't have any luck."

She sighed. "Nope. But maybe one of them will give me a call later."

"And you aren't going to be able to relax until you can tell them what you know, are you?" Hutch tucked the damp towel into the rack on the end of the counter before turning to her and putting both hands on her shoulder.

"Probably not."

He kissed her forehead. "Would you like to bounce some ideas off me? Would that help? I really can keep a secret."

"I know you can but I also know you don't like it when I get hung up on a case like this."

"I'm beginning to realize that I might as well get used to it."

"Oh, Hutch, I love you so much!"

"And I love you too. I must confess I'm ashamed of the way I've been acting."

"You're not the only guilty one here," Tempe said. "I have been neglecting you and Blair." Lowering her voice, she added, "Forgetting my own son's birthday...that's inexcusable."

"But understandable under the circumstances. If the Celsos had any idea how determined you are to bring their daughter's murderer to justice, they'd be so grateful."

"I'm not doing it for that reason."

He gently smoothed wisps of hair that had worked themselves loose from her braid, his fingers returning to cup her face. "I know you aren't. You just have to find out who the murderer is."

"I wouldn't care except those detectives just weren't looking beyond Daniel. And we both know Daniel didn't kill Marella."

"He has some big problems but I don't think killing that girl is one of them." He ran his index finger around the outline of her lips, his touch tingling all the way to her heart.

"And if they ever got around to talking to Isabel she wouldn't have told them what she knew about Marella." Her breathing quickened.

"But she did tell you." He pressed his lips against hers, kissing her slowly, lovingly.

Tempe closed her eyes, her body melding against his as his arms tightened around her. All thoughts of Marella's murder were replaced by this intense yearning for her husband.

"Is there time?" he whispered, his breath hot against her face.

"If we hurry," Tempe gasped. What did it matter if she were a few minutes late getting out into the field? She was always late getting home at the end of her shift.

"Hey, Mom!" Blair thundered down the hall and

burst into the kitchen. "There's a big fire out at the Whitcomb ranch. Thought you'd like to know!"

21

Blair's announcement shattered the moment. Tempe and Hutch pulled away from each other, her hand lingering on the small of his back, his touching her shoulder.

"Are you going out there?" Tempe asked.

"Of course," Blair said, his blond hair still damp from his shower. He pulled open the back door. "All my turn-out gear is in the car." And he was gone.

"I'm going too," Tempe said.

"But what about your job up here?" Hutch asked.

"I'll call the dispatcher and tell them to get a replacement for me until I get back."

Hutch followed her out to the Bronco. "I'm coming along."

"What about your sermon?" Tempe asked as she pulled herself into the driver's seat.

"I'll work on it in my head."

Tempe didn't give the dispatcher a chance to argue with her when she called in. "I'm on my way to a fire at the Whitcomb ranch. I won't make it back in time to start my shift in Bear Creek. Find someone to fill in for me." She signed off.

Long before they reached the Whitcomb's property, Hutch gasped, "Tempe, look!"

Billowing columns of smoke darkened the sky.

"It's a bad one."

The sound of sirens surrounded them. As they approached the boundaries of Whitcomb land, they came upon several cars parked along the road. Other volunteers. Blair's yellow VW was tucked in among them, though he was nowhere to be seen.

When they reached the open gate leading to the Whitcomb's house, she spotted a red water tender lumbering up the lane, with a smaller truck following. Riding on them were several figures wearing black helmets, jackets, trousers and boots all marked with wide fluorescent green stripes. No doubt one of them was Blair.

"I better leave the Bronco here. There's not all that much room up near the house for those engines to maneuver around. I know you aren't going to like this, Hutch, but I'd prefer it if you'd stay here." Tempe opened her door, heat hitting her like that coming from a blazing furnace. She slipped on her sunglasses.

Hutch rolled his window down but remained in his place. "I had a hunch you were going to say that. What are you going to do?"

"Head up there. Maybe I can hitch a ride. I want

to make sure the Whitcombs are all right."

"It kills me to let you just go like this. At least give me a kiss." Hutch leaned his head toward her. Just as they started to kiss, another fire truck came around the bend.

"I'll be fine. Say a prayer for the Whitcombs." She sprinted toward the gate just as the truck began its turn.

Waving her arms, she hollered, "Hey! Give me a ride up the hill, okay?" Before receiving an answer, Tempe jumped onto the running board, hooking her arm through the window.

"Welcome aboard, Deputy," the nearest fireman said.

Dust and smoke blew in Tempe's face as the truck labored up the steep, curving driveway. The already hot afternoon temperature had been raised by the fire. Tempe felt the sweat trickling down her back.

As they got closer to the top of the hill, the smoke thickened. It was impossible to see more than a few feet ahead. Tempe suspected one of the buildings was on fire.

She was right.

When they reached the flat area, Pete Roundtree, in regulation fire gear, appeared out of the thick, surging smoke and began shouting instructions to the new arrivals. Tempe jumped from her perch and looked around.

Flames leaped from the turrets of the Whitcomb's

castle house. Black smoke spiraled out of the upper windows. Firemen pointed hoses at the fire, the spray from the nozzles not seeming to have much effect.

Other fire fighters crisscrossed the open area, laying more hose, running around the building and disappearing into the engulfing black smoke. Tempe squinted against the stinging fumes, searching for signs of Grant Whitcomb and his sister.

Everyone was too busy to take any notice of Tempe as she jumped over hoses, darted around fire trucks, peered around the working men and a few women as she searched for the elderly siblings.

When she made her away around the burning structure, she spotted a tall figure using a shovel to throw dirt on new blazes in a grassy area. Even though a helmet covered his blond hair, and his turnout gear made his body bulky she knew it was Blair. Fire seemed to be everywhere. Working in the same capacity a few yards away was another familiar figure -- Daniel Redwing. Both young men were too involved in their work to notice her.

She recognized other faces--men and women she knew from Bear Creek working alongside Indians she'd seen at the Pow Wow, including Abel Contreras. But the Whitcombs were nowhere to be seen.

Tempe headed toward the barn, hoping they had taken refuge there. The large building didn't seem to be in any immediate danger from the many blazes.

The door of the barn was ajar. Tempe slipped inside, standing still for a moment to adjust to the dark interior. The scent of hay and manure had been permeated by the overpowering stench of the smoke.

Tempe was disappointed to find herself alone among various farm implements. "If the Whitcombs aren't here, where are they?"

Just as she decided to leave, Tempe noticed movement at the opposite end of the barn. "Who's there?" she called, thinking that it was probably some animal.

But when the far door was shoved open, and a dark haired man plunged through it, Tempe ran after him. "Hey, you! Stop!"

When she finally reached the door, she plunged out into thick smoke. Her first breath made her cough. She looked around trying to find the fleeing person. Men dressed in fire gear, and some without, darted around the fire scene. Deciding she couldn't pick out the person, Tempe started to walk down the hill. There was no purpose for her remaining at the scene; she'd just be in the way. It made more sense to keep Hutch company until Pete or someone else was free enough to talk to her.

She followed a path leading from the backside of the barn, cutting through the tall, dry grass. Though the smoke prevented her from seeing exactly where it went, she expected it to, at some point, intersect or at least come close to the lane.

Because the path was little more than an animal trail, the surface uneven and littered with rocks, she had to watch where she stepped. Not paying attention to anything but where she was going, she was surprised to hear the crackling sounds of a nearby fire.

Tempe jerked her head up. To the right of her the grass exploded into a brilliant display of sparks and flame. "Oh, dear God!"

Ahead, something moved across her path. The same dark haired man. But this time she was close enough to see him clearly. He was tall, his black hair shoulder length, his upper torso clad in a black T-shirt and a fringed leather vest. He was muscular without being bulky. As he ran, he carried a blazing torch. She knew he'd touched off the latest fire.

No longer even thinking about the unevenness of the path, Tempe galloped after the retreating figure. She didn't think he was yet aware that she followed him as he loped along at a medium pace.

He paused once to touch the torch to the grass. It ignited with an explosion, fire making it's way down the hill, consuming the dry vegetation.

Tempe pushed herself, wanting to catch up with him so she could stop him from lighting any more fires.

When she'd come near enough to tackle him, he finally became aware of her presence. He whirled around. It was Cody Endrezza. His black eyes opened in wide surprise. Recognition contorted his usual handsome features with hatred. "You!"

Unsnapping her holster, Tempe reached for her gun. "Stay right where you are, you are under arrest."

Cody threw the flaming torch at her like a spear, turned and darted off through the waist high growth.

Tempe leaped out of the way. The torch landed near her feet, immediately setting the grass on fire. At first Tempe thought she might be able to put it out as she stomped on the smoldering sparks. In seconds, they'd ignited into flames.

With the fire nipping at her heels and snapping like some sort of monstrous animal, Tempe ran as fast as she could. She no longer cared if she caught up with Cody, only that she keep ahead of the conflagration.

Sparks landed on her clothes; she brushed them away without missing a step.

Her attention was once again directed toward Cody. His vest was burning. He must have somehow ignited himself with the torch when he'd thrown it at her.

"Help me!" he screamed, flapping his arms and running in a circle, causing the flames devouring his clothing to spread.

"Drop down on the ground and roll!" Tempe hollered.

Cody ignored her as he plunged ahead wildly.

With a burst of speed, Tempe threw herself at him. She caught him around the knees, toppling him. Scrambling to her feet, Tempe turned him over, rolling him down the hill.

"Aghh!"

Tempe didn't know if Cody cried out in pain or

fear--though she suspected it might be a combination of both.

Though her action had squelched the flames on the vest, fire continued to rage all around them. In minutes they'd both be burning if she didn't act quickly. She remembered the pond. It couldn't be much farther ahead.

"Get up, Cody!" She yanked on his arm but he pulled away from her. "If you don't get up now we're going to be burned alive. Come on."

"Okay, okay." He lifted himself gingerly. When he realized the fire nearly surrounded them, his eyes widened in horror. "Oh, my God, what are we going to do?"

"There's a pond. If we can just reach it before the fire gets us we'll be safe. Let's go!" Tempe lunged ahead, feeling confident Cody would follow.

Though she had to run through the burning growth, the knowledge that safety lay somewhere ahead kept her going. She burst through a clump of dried thistles that had not yet caught fire, the sharp stickers catching her clothes.

Just ahead was the black surface of the pond. "We made it, Cody."

The fire began to circle around the water, the cattails on one edge burning like stately candles. Ignoring the green algae lining the edges, Tempe waded in. The water felt like a warm bath.

Cody plunged in, splashing water like a child at

play.

"Wade out into the middle," Tempe directed as the flames sped around the edges of the large pool. The rickety dock caught fire, in minutes it was completely engulfed. The row boat began to burn.

Tempe made her way toward Cody. The water reached her armpits. "Are you badly burned?"

"I don't know." Despite the heat from the fire and the warmth of the water, Cody began to shiver.

"I'm going to have to handcuff you." While he was still frightened was the best time to do it. He didn't resist as she brought his arms behind his back and snapped the cuffs around his wrists.

"Why did you set all these fires?" Tempe asked.

At first she didn't think he was going to answer. He continued staring at the blaze encircling them. Flames danced along the edges of the rowboat. "Didn't want old man Whitcomb to tell."

"Tell what?"

"That I stole his gun."

"How did you manage that, Cody?"

Sparks shot into the air causing Cody to flinch. "It was easy enough. I spotted that gun in his pocket and I kept watching him. He'd stand around glaring at what was going on, and then his eyes would kind of go out of focus. He didn't even seem to be there. I watched that happen two or three times during the day. Once when he was spaced out like that, I bumped against him. He didn't even notice. I just dipped my hand in his pocket and pulled out the gun. He came out of it just as I was walking away. He hollered, but didn't have the guts to come after me. I figured it was only a matter of time until he told you or someone else that he thought it was me that swiped his gun."

Tempe shook her head. "So you wanted the old man to burn up in his house."

"I just wanted to keep his mouth shut."

"And, of course, you're the one who shot Marella."

Pain was evident in his black eyes. "I didn't plan to do it. You've got to believe me."

"Why don't you tell me how it happened, Cody?"

The rowboat had nearly burned to the water line. The fire snapped and crackled all around the pond. The sky was black from the smoke and it was hard to breath.

"I loved Marella. I thought she loved me. I wanted to marry her." He coughed. "But she told me she didn't want to marry me...didn't want to see me anymore." He hung his head.

"What did you do, Cody?"

"The first time I saw her after she told me that was at the Pow Wow. I kept trying to talk to her. I pleaded with her to reconsider. Finally I asked her to come with me somewhere we could talk in private. She didn't want to, but I begged until she agreed. We went behind the exhibit hall. I told her again how much I loved her. Marella told me there was nothing I could say or do to make her change her mind."

"How did you feel then?"

"Angry. I was so angry! I thought maybe I could scare her into agreeing to marry me. I pulled the gun out and pointed it at her."

The fire burned all around the pond. Tempe and Cody were completely isolated as they waited together in the safety of the water.

22

Tempe waited for Cody to continue his confession.

"The gun went off. She didn't scream or anything. She just fell to the ground." He made a sound like a sob. "I knew she was dead. I tossed the gun and took off. Left the fairgrounds and didn't come back. I felt sick. Later on I went to see Marella's folks. They welcomed me with open arms. It was obvious she hadn't told them we'd broken up. I figured no one would guess I killed her."

"You left your calling card behind, the eagle feather," Tempe said.

"Anyone could have put it there," Cody said. He lifted his head, his belligerent attitude returning. Tempe was glad she'd already cuffed him.

"But the feather belonged to you. It fell off your dance outfit."

Since they weren't going anywhere until the fire passed, Tempe decided to clear up another question.

"You were the one that shot at me yesterday, weren't you?"

"I knew it was just a matter of time before you figured everything out. You couldn't leave things alone. All the time, sticking your nose in where it didn't belong. While I was scouting old man Whitcomb's place, I spotted you talking to Katherine Davelos down there by the river. Knew it wouldn't be long before she told you she'd seen me that night."

"When did she see you, Cody?" Tempe prompted.

He shrugged. "Right after I shot Marella. When I was coming out of the gate. She looked right at me."

"She told me it was Daniel Redwing she saw."

Cody laughed humorlessly. "I think she has some crazy idea about fixing me up with her daughter."

Crazy was right! Katherine must suspect Cody had killed Marella. Would she really want her own child involved with a murderer? It no doubt had something to do with the fact that Cody was a lead dancer which in Katherine's warped mind instilled him with more value than Daniel Redwing. Tempe's sympathy for Linda grew.

"When you saw Katherine and me together, you decided to do away with both of us."

"No, no." Cody pulled away from her. "I just wanted to give you a scare. The straw hat and limp were a good touch, don't you think?" He chuckled, which started a coughing fit.

Finally burning itself out, the fire left a scattering

of red coals sparkling on a background of smoldering ashes.

"Time to get out of here," Tempe said, grabbing Cody by his elbow. Tempe sloshed her way to the bank, guiding the reluctant young man. "You're under arrest for the murder of Marella Celso. You have the right to remain silent. Anything you say can and...." Tempe finished the recitation as they scrambled up onto the bank.

"Where we going now?" Cody asked. Water dripped from them both. The charred ground sizzled.

"I'm taking you to the substation." Tempe pulled him along as she made her way toward the lane.

Upon reaching it, she was halted by the sound of her husband's voice shouting from the top of the next rise. "Tempe, Tempe. Wait for me!"

Keeping her grip on Cody's upper arm, Tempe watched Hutch run down the hill towards her. When he got closer, his eyes widened as he looked her over.

"Thank God you're safe. I thought sure you'd been burned to death! You look a mess...no, no, you look wonderful! What happened?"

Glancing down she saw black-edged burn holes on her khaki shirt and pants. From her chest down, she dripped water. "Been busy catching Marella's murderer."

"Cody killed Marella?" Hutch sounded incredulous.

"That's right." She rubbed her free hand on her

cheek, it came away sooty. "Where were you? I thought I asked you to wait in the Bronco."

Hutch grinned. "I got tired of waiting. Hitched a ride just like you did. Looked all over for you. One of the firemen said he spotted you chasing someone down the hill. When I started after you, the whole area burst into flames. I was desperate so I dropped to my knees and started praying.

"I told Pete you were down there, but he said he didn't have the manpower or the water to do anything about that section of the fire. A line of firefighters prevented the flames from crossing into reservation land, and the captain said the fire would go out when it reached the road. All I could imagine was the worst."

Ignoring Cody, Hutch took Tempe into his arms. "Thank God you're all right. How did you escape that fire storm?"

"Cody and I waited it out in the pond."

"Oh, yes. I forgot all about the pond."

"Glad I didn't."

They began walking down the lane toward the Bronco. Hutch put his arm around Tempe's waist while Tempe hung onto Cody. "Did you hear anything about the Whitcombs? Are they all right?" she asked.

"Grant is in the hospital. Smoke inhalation. Pete didn't think it was too serious."

"I'm glad to hear it. What about Alice?"

"She was taken to the reservation."

Cody rode in the back of the Bronco. Hutch sat

beside her as she drove toward town, his arm draped around her shoulder.

Tempe contacted the dispatcher. "I'm bringing in Marella Celso's murderer. Let Sergeant Guthrie know."

Guthrie was waiting for them on the porch of the sub-station. When Tempe climbed out of the Bronco, the sergeant's eyes opened wide. "What the hell happened to you?"

"Got caught in a fire," Tempe said.

"The one out at the reservation?" Guthrie looked from her to Cody and back again.

"That's right," Tempe said, pushing Cody ahead of her up the steps of the porch.

Guthrie glowered at her. "What is this bit about you calling in asking for someone to cover for you? Who gave you the authority to do that?"

Before Tempe could answer, Hutch squeezed by her and her prisoner. Standing directly in front of the Sergeant, he said quietly, "Excuse me, Sergeant Guthrie, but I think you need to be reminded that my wife solved this murder case for you."

Tempe grinned at her husband. Looking uncomfortable, the Sergeant cleared his throat. "Yes...well...there is that. Take care of the suspect, Crabtree. When you're done, come to my office for a de-briefing."

After Cody was booked she turned him over to another deputy to transport him to the emergency room to have his burns treated. Tempe took the time to wash her face and rebraid her hair before rejoining Hutch where he waited just outside the door. "Too bad you don't have your own car," she said.

Grinning, Hutch slung his arm around her shoulder. "I wouldn't have missed this for the world. It's like getting to be in on the fitting together of the final pieces of a puzzle. Something I usually only hear about."

Tempe paused at the open door to Sergeant Guthrie's office. The Sergeant looked up from the papers he'd been scanning. "Have a seat, Crabtree." After noticing Hutch right beside her, he added, "You too, Pastor."

"I'm happy standing." Hutch crossed his arms and leaned against the door frame.

Tempe guessed that he intended to appear menacing though he merely looked uncomfortable. However, she was touched by his effort to help her. She smiled at him before sitting opposite the sergeant.

Obviously not intimidated by Hutch's stance, Sergeant Guthrie leaned back in his chair, focusing his attention on Tempe. "Tell me everything beginning with why you requested a replacement for your shift."

Hutch cleared his throat.

"When I heard about the big fire on Grant Whitcomb's ranch, I decided to go out there. Since it was nearly time for my shift to begin, I notified the dispatcher to send someone up to Bear Creek to take my place."

"Uh huh." Guthrie didn't have to say anything more for Tempe to know he didn't think that was an adequate excuse for her action.

"When I arrived on the scene the Whitcombs' home was totally involved. I began searching for Grant Whitcomb and his sister without any luck. But while I was looking I spotted someone acting suspiciously. It turned out to be Cody Endrezza fleeing the fire area. As I followed he set more fires. Before I could stop him, he accidentally caught himself on fire."

"Must not have done too much damage," Guthrie said.

"Only because I was able to knock him down and put the fire out. He's being checked out now at emergency."

"Go on with your story."

"We were both threatened by the flames and managed to reach a large pond. While we waited for the fire to pass, Cody confessed that he murdered Marella."

"Tell me about that."

Tempe explained in detail everything Cody had related to her about how and why he'd killed Marella.

The sergeant took notes but when she'd finished, he added, "I know the detectives will want to hear all of this from you."

"I'll be glad to tell them. But right now I'd like to get going. If you don't mind, Sergeant, I'm going to take the rest of the night off." She stood.

Guthrie's bushy eyebrows met for a moment. He looked as though he'd like to argue with her but thought better of it. "All right, Crabtree."

When they reached the Bronco, Hutch asked, "Why do I get the feeling you aren't ready to go home?" The night air was still oppressively hot.

"Because you know how I think." Tempe unlocked the passenger door for her husband and went around to the driver's side.

"So where are we going?" Hutch asked as he fastened his seat belt.

"I want to be the first to tell the Celsos the news."

Even though Tempe had scrubbed the soot from her face and fixed her hair, Violet Celso gasped when she opened the door to her knock.

"My goodness, Deputy, are you all right?"

Glancing down at her stained and burned uniform, Tempe said, "I'm fine. I have some news. May we come in?"

Violet held the door wide, curiosity apparent on her round, weathered face. As they entered, Jake, who had been sitting on a recliner facing the television, jumped to his feet.

"What's wrong? More bad news."

Tempe wasn't sure how they'd take what she had to report. "Why don't you both sit down?"

Violet backed up until she reached her husband. They huddled together on the couch. Hutch and Tempe remained standing.

"I arrested Marella's murderer today," Tempe said.

"Finally got enough evidence on that Redwing kid to put him behind bars." Jake held both his wife's hands.

"Daniel Redwing didn't have anything to do with your daughter's death."

"Please don't keep us in suspense, Deputy," Violet said. "Who killed Marella?"

There was no easy way to break the news. "Cody Endrezza confessed to shooting her."

Violet cried out as if in pain. Her husband growled, "I don't believe it. What reason would he have to kill her?"

"You did know that Marella was pregnant, didn't you?"

Jake hung his head. In a small voice, Violet said, "Yes, we were told."

"The baby was Cody's."

Violet nodded. "I was sure of that."

"But Marella didn't want to marry Cody."

"I find that very difficult to believe. She was crazy about him."

"It's true," Tempe said. "Something happened between them. Marella changed her mind. She didn't want to marry him and that's why Cody killed her. I don't think he planned to do it, it just happened."

"I don't understand why she didn't tell us any of this. About being pregnant...breaking up with Cody. We would have helped her any way we could." Violet began to cry and Jake put his arms around her.

"I'm positive she would have confided in you eventually," Tempe said, shifting from one foot to the other.

"Are you sure about all this? Cody loved Marella. I'm having trouble accepting the fact he killed her," Jake said.

"Yes, I'm sure. He confessed. And he's the one who set fire to the Whitcombs' house."

"That fire nearly killed Grant Whitcomb," Jake said, shaking his head sadly.

"That was Cody's intention. He stole Grant's gun and was afraid he might tell someone."

"Oh, my God," Violet groaned.

"Whitcomb's sister is here. We put her to bed in Marella's room," Jake offered.

It was Tempe's turn to be surprised. "After all Grant Whitcomb has done to you, you're caring for his sister?"

"I'm sure your husband understands," Violet said.

Hutch circled Tempe's shoulder. "Just like Jesus, turning the other cheek."

Violet nodded. "And in the Indian way, it shows our interdependency upon one another."

"We'll have to do something to make up for the dark thoughts we had about Daniel Redwing." Jake stood.

"I hoped that's what you would want to do. Daniel needs help with his drinking problem. A strong male role model would do him a lot of good," Hutch said.

Leaning against her husband, Violet smiled. "Don't worry, Pastor. We'll tend to Daniel. I'm sure Jake will know exactly what to do."

As Tempe backed the Bronco down the Celsos' hill, Hutch said, "Where to now?"

"I have one more stop. I want to return Mrs. Redwing's gun. I'm sure both Daniel and Isabel will be relieved to know Cody has been arrested for Marella's murder."

Even though it was dark, Tempe could see her husband's smile. "That's still not all, is it."

"I would like to check on the fire scene. See if they've got it all out. Find out how Blair is doing."

Hutch put his hand over hers on the steering wheel. He didn't say anything, he didn't have to.

The End